REBOUND O

WHEN ESSEX

F.W. RIDER

DEDICATION

For my gorgeous husband, my biggest supporter and my
Main Man all the live long day!
Rebound On The Ranch
Written by
F. W. Rider
If you'd like to find out more about forthcoming releases or
the life of my equine army in general, check out my links
below! You can also read my previous releases via the links
below…

Get to know me more here…
Instagram - https://www.
instagram.com/thefairweatherrider/
Facebook - https://www.facebook.com/thefairweatherrider
Website - http://thefairweatherrider.com

Due to the rather excessive use of profanity, graphic sexual
references and adult subject matter, this book should only be
read by those who aren't easily offended and should without
a doubt be kept out of reach of anyone under the age of 18.

REBOUND ON THE RANCH

Written By
F.W. Rider

Contact info@thefairweatherrider.com for more
information on future releases.

ALICE

I can feel the paranoia coming over me in waves. It's ridiculous. I feel like a complete loser, feeling so vulnerable and worrying so much about what others are currently thinking of me, but I can't shake the suspicion that everyone knows what's just happened. I'm crammed into this toddler-sized economy seat with my hand luggage between my feet. I'm doing it – I'm going. I'm leaving behind all the shit and doing what I always wanted to do, yet despite this, here I am, worried that someone can read the word 'mug' written across my forehead.

What's funny – and I can almost feel myself stifle an astounded giggle as I say this – but if this had happened to a friend, I'd have picked up on things long ago. More to the point, I would have never dreamt of trying to *fix things* and instead told them, 'Get rid and find someone better.'

He bloody well did it, didn't he? Cheated on me. Wasn't just a one-night stand or a short affair. Oh no. When Alex does things, he doesn't do them by halves. He went for the full blown three-year-long affair, living a double life that even his parents helped him keep under wraps.

I cannot for the life of me make any sense of it. He had everything: a great career, a great group of friends. Bloody hell, I thought we even had a pretty great relationship, doing what we both loved – working with horses. I put everything – all the dreams I'd had in my late teens and early twenties of travelling the world – on hold for him. I put everything aside so he could focus on his showjumping, and he absolutely shat on me.

I could just imagine if the likes of Jen had come to me and asked, 'This guy is behaving in such and such a way – what do you think?' I'd have given her the toughest love I could muster before throttling the guy who'd dared to mess her around. But when it happened to me?

God, I shudder just thinking about how pathetic I sounded.

'Was it my fault? Did I push you to do this?'

'Do you not fancy me anymore?'

'Do you want me to make more of an effort?'

I don't recognise myself anymore. I truly don't know who I am when I look in the mirror.

For years, I'd wanted to gain experience within the equestrian world, venturing away from showjumping and exploring the world of equestrianism in every aspect, every discipline. Yes, I absolutely love low-level showjumping and eventing. It gives me a true thrill, but what I love more than the sport is the horse itself. And not just the horse or the equine species but the psychology of the animal. I can spend hours watching wild horses interacting on YouTube, because let's face it, you're never going to see that here in Brentwood.

I love watching the way these animals communicate with each other, and more interestingly, I love watching how a horse will try to communicate with a human, only for it to be completely unheard ninety-nine per cent of the time. I had all sorts of wild dreams about heading to the States and working on a ranch with the mustangs that come in to be 'gentled'. But instead of pursuing that while I was young and child-free, I chose instead to be the dutiful girlfriend who accompanied my up-and-coming showjumper boyfriend on the circuit – when I wasn't looking after his horses back home.

To be quite honest, there were times when I wondered if I wanted more, but a few sweet, whispered words and I became putty in his manipulative hands.

I found out he was cheating on me through a mutual acquaintance. She was never more than that for the simple fact that she wanted to be with him. It was the age-old cliché of your boyfriend having a female best friend and her doing all she could to break us up. I'm sure the day she found out he was having an affair felt like all of her birthdays and Christmases had come at once. The joy on her condescending face is a picture I'll never get out of my head. On my worst days, I imagine doing something that will wipe that smug-arse look straight off of her face before having to remind myself that I'm better than that. I hate her. But I'm determined to move on. To go and do what I was always supposed to do with my life. Live it.

Hence finding myself here, surrounded by strangers on a plane to the Orange City ranch in Utah. To date, there are supposed to be over twenty herds of wild horses on Utah public land. They're absolutely cherished by the people of Utah, but the Bureau of Land Management fear a wild horse problem through overbreeding. Just a little while ago, they commissioned helicopters to round them up in holding pens where over four hundred stallions, mares and foals were captured. Just over a hundred mares were given fertility-control injections and the rest, around three hundred or so, were sent to a holding facility to enter permanent captivity as domesticated wild horses. The Orange City ranch are known for their incredible horse-training program, led by the super talented Noah Williams. His parents were trainers and their parents before them. Orange City has become such as well-known training facility, around the world in fact, that when I finally came to my senses about Alex, I knew exactly what I had to do.

It boggles the mind how easily I was willing to give up my dreams for him, especially as I feel the fire inside of me now, sitting on this plane.

The man next to me keeps throwing filthy looks my way. I think it might have something to do with my constant knee twitching and fidgeting. Trying to contain myself and calm my extremities before he physically removes me from the plane mid-air, I think back to the only reason I considered not flying – the horses.

Alfie and Jack are my heavies. My boys. Alfie is a pure-bred Clydesdale. He was a troublesome boy, handed in to my local rescue, underweight and with a mean temper on him. But after a little love and attention, and the right food, he came round pretty quickly. It was Jack who gave me the biggest problems. Jack had been given a pretty rough start in his life. He'd been beaten to a pulp, the poor sod, so his attitude to people by the time I got my hands on him wasn't the best, but who could blame him?

He took a while to come round. We spent a lot of time in the field, me just sat on the ground, gaining his trust as he grazed. I'm proud to say that after a few near misses, some bruises and one broken arm – thanks, Jack – we're closer than I could have ever imagined. He isn't a huge fan of other people and that's fine.

I've backed the both of them, though Jack was beaten so badly that I don't feel he's fully comfortable with a saddle on. As a result, the pair of them live the life of luxury in their grazing field, enjoying long grass and acres to roam as they please. They come in to have their hooves picked out and a brush down, though not too in-depth – I don't want them to lose their oils. But they have everything they need, and I couldn't be happier. I feel immense pride when I think of the pair of them. I wonder how they're doing, but I know they're both being well looked after by Mum while I'm gone so I needn't worry.

As I hear yet another tut from the man next to me, I look up and catch the tail end of the pilot's announcement.

'We're beginning our descent into Salt Lake City International.'

I've done it. I'm here. I'm about to embark on the adventure of a lifetime training wild mustangs and ensuring they find the right homes, something I feel I'm currently without.

Despite that, and despite the nerves and current self-confidence issues I'm facing, I'm feeling rather positive about this next move. After speaking with Noah Williams' parents, who still own the ranch, I was put at ease straight away. They were so warm over the phone. I can't actually believe I got the gig, to be honest. I thought I'd be on a waiting list for months, if not years, but I was lucky enough to nab a space straight away. After briefly wandering off in my mind to consider why I'm not on a wait list and why there isn't a flock of people lining up to work with Noah, I'm knocked to by the *bing-bong* of the seat belt reminder.

I can feel the plane begin to descend and see the passengers' attitudes begin to change. Some get anxious as they feel the pressure change, others get impatient as soon as they hear the word 'descent' and some just look plain miserable. I wonder if anyone else is on a similar journey to me. A new adventure. Something that's going to be life changing.

Working under Noah, I hope to learn a way of training that I simply haven't been able to access, take what I learn back to the UK and maybe one day open my own training facility. Alex may have laughed, but maybe now I'll have the last laugh. Who knows?

I spot the air hostess. She smiles sweetly, the same reassuring smile she must dish out to just about every traveller.

Here we go. Essex is about to meet Utah and I'm so bloody excited.

NOAH

'We don't need anyone here, Ma. I don't need any help. I've told you this for months.'

I don't like getting annoyed with my parents. Without them, I just don't know where I'd be, but hell, I don't need some woman from the UK following me around like a bad stink.

'Why are you being so moody? I think it'll be fun!' Annabelle looks at me with the same excitement I see when I suggest going for ice cream. Since her mum departed, it's just been me, her and her grandparents here. She goes to school Monday through Friday, on the school bus, apart from today – she's heading in extra early to get in some additional cheer practice. Though she's only six, she could very well be sixteen and I wouldn't see a difference in her attitude or the way she carries herself.

It amazes me just how wise she can be sometimes. She doesn't get that from her mum, that's for sure.

'Honey, we need help. You're getting busier and busier with people sending their competition horses from all over the country, and we have thirty-five mustangs arriving tomorrow. There is no way that you're gonna be able to deal with all of those and have time for Annabelle. You need to be sensible here, Noah.' She's almost pleading with me.

I huff, indignant, but I know she's right. I have trouble saying no, whether that's to my daughter or a client. I want to be able to please everyone, but as word broke out that I wasn't just working with mustangs and had helped a few locals, my business boomed. Soon enough, I was being contacted from all over the country – people as far as California wanted to send their horses to me. I enjoy it, I really do, but with the mustangs coming tomorrow, I know I'm going to need help. I just wish my parents had let me arrange it, though I guess if they had, I would have turned just about everyone away. They think I need help with the mustangs and the barn work. I think differently, and I guess I'm a little picky.

So here I am, arguing with my 65-year-old mother, a man of thirty-eight. I may as well stomp my feet and throw my toys on the ground – I'm acting like a baby. I just need to suck it up. I will. I'll get past it and get things done for the farm, for Annabelle. It'll probably do her some good to be fair. Aside from school, we're all she sees on our five-hundred-acre farm. She loves her life, but I do wonder whether she'd be happier with some more company. Although, whether she will or won't be is irrelevant considering I'm going to pick up this woman today.

They said her name was Alice Humphries. I checked her out on social media and by the looks of it, she works with heavy horses but nothing that can move. I mean, she showjumps and events, but that's about it. She does something called team chasing too. I'm not sure what that is, but I haven't seen much evidence of her working with wild horses or even horses with any kind of issue. I think, in all honestly, she'll be best being put to work in the barn and leaving it there.

Mum cocks her head at me before raising an eyebrow. I know she means business now. I also know better than to keep on and just accept my fate – babysitting a new, albeit temporary, farmhand.

'Where's Annabelle got to? She was right here a second ago? Doesn't she want to get to school super early or something?' I look at my mom, who's currently standing in the doorway, looking behind her. I can hear rustling and my daughter's high-pitched voice shouting 'I love ya' to her grandpa. She's a good kid. She's had a lot to deal with in her young life, but she's handled it all like a pro.

I don't know where I'd be without her, but I do know she's my main purpose in life. Making sure she's happy and healthy. I might be a single parent now, but I like to think I'm doing OK.

I walk back to the barn to grab one last bale of hay. I figure I've got an hour between dropping Annabelle off at school and picking up this Alice chick, so I may as well drop some hay off for the horses in the fields near her school before I head to the airport.

I throw the last bale into the pickup. It bounces once then lands neatly in the gap between the two bales either side of it. 'It's as if I've done this a million times before,' I mouth to myself.

I head round to the left-hand side and spot Annabelle bouncing down the steps, half dressing herself, half trying to keep her backpack on. I spot the last half of a donut in her mouth too, which I'm guessing her soft-as-shit grandpa let her have right after she told him she loved him.

I roll my eyes and slide in the driver's seat. There's no use trying to argue now. This has been going on for the last six years, and I'm sure it'll continue for many more to come. Annabelle has a special relationship with her grandpa, one that I wouldn't ever want to mess with, especially over the odd donut or two. The kid's going to be on a serious sugar high from here to school. Her teachers won't know what's hit them.

As the door on Annabelle's side closes, I wave my mom goodbye and give my baby the side eye to make sure she's putting her seat belt on before I knock the truck into drive and get going. We're not even halfway down the drive before I'm trying to dust hay and crap off the seats.

'Daddy, I'm fine. We're farmers. It's OK if I have a little hay on my clothes when I get to school.'

'We may be farmers, sweetie, but that doesn't give you an excuse to look messy when you turn up to school. It's important to make a good impression on people, and having hay in your hair before you've even arrived at school is the best way to make a bad impression.'

She rolls her eyes at me. Definitely gets that from me…

'So what's Alice like?'

'How do you know her name?'

'Grandma told me about her. Said she's a horse trainer from En-Ger-Land!' She accentuates every syllable of the word and I can't help but smile at her excitement.

'Is she gonna be a real posh lady?'

'I don't know about that, but what I do know is regardless of how she talks, she's no better than you.'

Cue another eye roll from the apparent pre-teen. 'Daddy, are you excited to have another lady on the farm? You might get a girlfriend.'

'What do you know about girlfriends? I have no time for them anyway. You're the woman in my life and that's that.

Besides, I don't know if she's going to be training horses, but I do know she'll be helping out in the barn, which means less work for me and more time with you. That's a bonus in my eyes. I miss being with you as much since work started getting busy. I like spending time with you and hearing about your day, and I don't feel like I've got to do a lot of that.'

'That's OK, Daddy. You have to work, right?'

'Right… but that doesn't make it OK. I have to find a balance.'

'What's a balance? Like balancing on a balance beam?'

'A little. Imagine I'm on a balance beam and I have a huge stick in my hands. On each end of that stick is a ball. One ball has work written on it and one ball has Annabelle written on it…'

'That's me!'

'That's right. Sometimes though, especially lately, that work ball has been getting heavier than my Annabelle ball. That means sometimes I can get a little…'

'Wobbly?'

'Something like that. Anyway, I'm going to try to make sure both of those balls are the same so I don't… wobble so much. I promise I'm trying, and this girl from England is going to help with that, OK?'

'OK, sounds good to me.' She smiles that winning smile that works every single time and kills me just a little. She looks so much like her mum when she does.

No sooner have I pulled up to the school than she's unbuckling herself and sprinting off to the school doors as if we never had a single conversation the whole journey. I hear a faint 'Love ya, Daddy' and she's gone through the class doors, screaming as she meets a friend. I'm luckier than I'll ever realise with that kid.

I look at my watch – there's still a good fifty minutes

before I need to be at the airport so I swing the truck back around and head to a field that marks the very furthest point of our land. I have three mustangs there I worked with last year. I intend to bring them back into work at the end of this year – if I ever get time – to find them new homes. They need a job to keep those brains ticking over. They deserve more than to just be field ornaments.

They hear my truck before they see me, and I hear their nickering too. They got friendly with me kinda quick, which was a real confidence boost when I needed it the most last year. The three of them wander over – two chestnut mares and a black gelding that's as dark as night. He's beautiful. So black that he doesn't even bleach in the sun. His coat really is unreal, and he's rare too. You don't see many black mustangs. I always thought about keeping him for myself, but if I don't have time for Annabelle, I sure as hell don't have time for more horses.

'Hey, you guys – I got your hay. Got some pellets in the back too.'

The wind is starting to pick up, and the temperature's beginning to drop too. They'll need a little extra feed through the winter considering they aren't roaming thousands of acres with unlimited grass, so the sooner I can find them new homes, the better coz they're currently costing me money I don't need to be spending. I guess I've been putting it off because of him – Onyx as I call him.

I toss the hay in sections as I walk through the field and then sprinkle the pellets too. They follow me for the pellets first. They'll go back to the hay once they've polished those off.

Giving them all a quick check, I run my hands over them all, checking hooves, legs, eyes and then their bodies. Once I'm happy they're all looking good, I start making my way back to the truck. One of the chestnut mares starts following me until a particular pellet takes her fancy and she decides that's more interesting than me.

I slide into my seat and make my way out onto the road, heading toward the airport. It's a good forty-minute drive but I have my tunes and the open road. It's all good right now.

NOAH

I pull into the pick-up point at arrivals. I had to fill up with gas and figured it was only polite to grab a couple of drinks. I got my usual black coffee and I got her the only thing I thought she might like – English breakfast tea. I know I said I didn't want her coming to the farm, but I'm not an asshole. My parents said she'd never been here before so I guess I have to give her a good ol' Utah welcome.

I'm waiting no more than five minutes before I see a beautiful woman, tall and strong but nervous looking. I'm shocked at how attractive she is. She's standing on the side-walk looking at all the cars and has a suitcase next to her with a backpack over her shoulder.

She's shivering. I guess she did what most tourists do and assumed it's always hot in America.

She has a thin denim jacket over a vest top and leggings with sneakers. She does not look ready to be hitting the farm, but my God, she looks good.

Tall and slim but strong. Her hair is dark and it instantly reminds me of Onyx. The shine is eye-catching. Damn. I haven't looked at a woman like this in a long time.

What the hell is going on with me?

She turns and catches me staring and instantly looks away before her gaze flits back quickly. I adjust in my seat and open the car door. She watches me, looking more nervous than she did before as I exit the truck and quietly but assertively put out a hand.

'Hiya. I'm Alice. You must be Noah... well I know you're Noah obviously because I've followed your career, but it almost feels weird, doesn't it, knowing someone before you've ever met them? Not that I know you. I don't *know* you, but I know of you I guess. If that makes any sense? At all? Does it? Please say something before I carry on. I will carry on. I hate awkward silences.'

'I'm Noah. Pleased to meet you.' I can't help but remain a little stand-offish. I feel caught off guard and, if I'm honest, a little flustered by how attracted I am to her.

'OK.' She's notably taken aback by the cold front coming from me, even worse than the Utah chill.

I stick my other hand out and offer her the cup, still remaining quiet but keeping a hold of her gaze.

'I got you an English tea. I didn't know if you wanted sugar so I have a couple sachets in the truck. It's getting pretty cold here. Do you have a coat? Thicker than that?' And I nod to the jean jacket without realising I'm now staring at her breasts.

'I've got plenty of sugar, as you can no doubt see. You had quite enough of a look now?'

I look up to see a face that's no longer nervous and now a little pissed off. Damn, she looks hotter when she's mad.

'Right, I apologise. I was just thinking about a coat. Unless you've got one in that suitcase. But I have a spare you can wear. Might be a little big on you, but it'll do for the month you're here.'

'Yeah I bet...' she mutters out the corner of her mouth. Damn, she's feisty.

I head to the driver's door and find her standing next to me.

She blushes before walking round to the other side of the truck and letting herself in. 'I forget you drive on the opposite side of the road over here, right?' And just like that, her anger dissipates into a coy, nervous expression once more. Still hot. God damn.

I pull out and have to slam on the brakes to avoid the car I clearly didn't bother to look for. I'm nervous, for crying out loud. She lets out a tiny gasp and grabs hold of the door handle.

'Sorry about that. I should have seen that. I'm a safe driver, honest.' I give a little smile, which thankfully she reciprocates.

'So I'm looking forward to working with you. Like I blabbed earlier, I've followed your career for a long time. I'm so excited to be training with you.'

'Training with me?'

'Yeah, you know, following you around and watching you at work and helping you with the mustangs you have arriving tomorrow. I've been training hors—'

'Listen, I don't need any help with training. I don't need help running the farm. A little help in the barn maybe, mucking out, etc., but I definitely don't need help with the training. That's my thing; I have a certain way of doing things. I certainly don't need your help in that department, and as much as I'd love to help you further your own training, I don't have the time to be teaching you while I'm training the mustangs or my clients' horses.'

'Hang on a minute. When I spoke to – I presume – your parents, they said they were looking for someone with my previous experience to help with the mustangs and any other horses you might want help with. I didn't fly thousands of miles to shovel shit. I could have done that back home in Essex.'

'Essex? That's where you're from? Don't they have that programme… what do they call it? *TOWIE*? Now I recognise your accent.'

'I couldn't give a rat's arse about some dodgy TV show or my accent. I spent thousands of pounds on a flight out here and now I've arrived, you're giving it "no thank you, ma'am" – I don't bloody think so!'

I flick my gaze toward her, my eyes wide. I can't believe the attitude coming off of her right now. From being a nervous thing on the sidewalk, now I see fire in her body, fire in her soul.

'Listen, this is my farm—'

'No, actually, it's your parents' farm and they're the ones who've invited me here for training. Bloody hell, all these years I thought you were such an incredible man and now within ten minutes of meeting you, I find out you're an arrogant, rude fucking lech.'

'Now wait a minute – I am none of those things.'

'Oh get stuffed.' And she crosses her arms defiantly before turning her head to look out the window.

Wow, I've really handled this one badly and more than likely come across as a huge lecherous asshole. Fuck.

The rest of the ride back to the farm is in awkward silence. I glance at her every now and then but get nothing back. I have a distinct idea that the reaction I got wasn't entirely aimed at me, though I can't deny I deserved it, but I definitely know I'm in for a month of trouble.

ALICE

*I*t feels like we're pulling along the driveway for an age. This farm is huge. It's vast and open. I can't believe the amount of hills I see in front of me. It's everything I imagined it to be and more. It's just a shame I have to share it with this absolute toss pot. All those hours I've spent dreaming about meeting Noah Williams, my idol. And here we are sat in a truck not talking because apparently he's sticking me on shit-shovelling duty for a fucking month.

What the hell did I do, coming out here? As much as I'd love to simply turn back around and leave him open-mouthed – he was quite shocked at my earlier rebuttal – the thought of going back home to Alex doesn't fill me with any greater sense of comfort.

I've yet to switch my phone back on. It would probably be a good idea, especially as my parents were rather worried at my sudden decision to leave everything and fly across the world to train with a complete stranger.

I switch it on while we're still heading along the lane to their home, and in an instant the screen lights up with messages from everyone from my parents to Jen and then him. Absolute wanker.

I can see Noah glancing at me before looking back to the road. He can get stuffed too. Men. I've honestly had it up to here with their controlling, deceitful ways.

I delete the message without reading it and let my parents know I've landed safe and am just pulling up at the farmhouse.

The house itself is old and rustic but quite simply beautiful. It's the same one you can see on his website but a tad more weather-beaten. The barns to the left are huge and open-ended. I can see some horses are in there munching away on their hay, ears pricked as the truck's engine is turned off.

Before I can get out and grab my suitcase and backpack, Noah is round at my door opening it for me. I mutter a thank you to the ground and walk to the back of the truck, throwing my backpack over my shoulder. Before I can grab my suitcase, he has it in his hands and is lifting it over the back of the truck, dusting some hay off it.

'Sorry about the hay. It looks pretty expensive – you wouldn't want to get it all mucked up.'

'It's a suitcase. Its job is to protect what's inside of it, not look pretty.'

He seems pretty shocked by my response, perhaps associating me with the girls of *TOWIE* and an inability to get my hands dirty.

'Well, still, just because you work on a farm doesn't mean you need to dress like you do. I like to keep my things clean, not that my truck would have you think that, but I do. It's something I like to teach my daughter.'

'You have a daughter? How old is she?'

'She's six but acts about sixteen.'

'Yeah, we all do that at that age, right? My younger sister was exactly the same.'

'And what's she like now?'

'Umm, she passed away when she was fifteen. She would have been twenty-three now. I just remember calling her a "threenager" when she was a toddler, and she just got more attitude from there. She was funny. Super spunky. You wouldn't mess with her.'

I look around the farm, feeling warmth at the thought of my younger sister, though her death almost broke our family.

My parents struggled to cope, but they did eventually. It was a hard time, but we got through it. I have her picture in my locket so I can carry a piece of her everywhere.

If I'm honest, it was Izzy's memory that helped me leave Alex. I remember feeling so pathetic, sitting alone on my bed and wondering what to do. The thought of leaving him was agony, and then I caught a glimpse of her picture on my wall. It felt like she was staring at me. God, she was gutsy. She never suffered fools and took no prisoners when it came to telling people what she thought. Even when she was ill. In the photo, her face is squished up next to mine. We're sitting in a hospital ward, both of us smiling, sucking on ice lollies as she's having her chemo.

She carried on smiling and carried on being as sarcastic as ever right until the end. It made me realise she wouldn't have put up with any of Alex's shit and, more to the point, she wouldn't have put up with me taking his shit, trying to change myself, blaming myself.

She would have given me a slap, insisted I sort myself out and then absolutely gone for this throat. At that moment, I'd jumped online and inquired about coming here.

I knew what I had to do. I collected my things from his place the next day while he was either at work or with her and refused to answer his calls. He was too gutless to come to my house, I think for fear of my father's wrath. It was a little over a week, sorting the horses and packing my things, before I was gone. I figured I didn't need to give Alex notice of my leaving considering he was preoccupied with someone else.

He had a tonne of people who clung to his every word, wanting to help and grab some small piece of his showjumping stardom, and he loved every minute of it. I'm sure one of them could step in for me.

I look up from my bags, after having been submerged within my own thoughts, to find Noah staring at me, a blank expression on his face. He, like many people, doesn't know what to say. It's not something everyone goes through, losing their sibling, their best friend when they're eighteen. She was my soulmate, but I've dealt with it better than I thought I would. I try to live my life for her, to make sure she's proud. I was and always will be a non-believer, but I sometimes wonder if she is looking down on me, perhaps wondering what the fuck I was doing with Alex, who the hell I'd become, though right now, she'd be fist-pumping with pride at me being bold enough to leave and go on this wild, if slightly unexpected adventure.

'I'm sorry to hear that.'

'It wasn't your fault so there's no need to be sorry. I can take my bags, thank you.'

As I grab my suitcase and walk past him, I'm greeted with the wet nose of a German shepherd. He's all ears and feet. He's young too and full of energy. I know I'm going to fall in love with him instantly.

I drop my bags and bend down to meet him instead of letting him continue to sniff my crotch. Between that and having Noah staring at my tits, I'm getting the feeling these guys are a very open bunch.

As I'm giving the dog a good ear rub and letting him lick my cheeks, I glance around some more, seeing a small circular corral as well as a large – I'm guessing thirty by forty – arena. Then there's the horse walker, great for letting off energy, though I'm surprised to see it here. I don't recall any mention of it on his website and wonder whether he keeps it solely for the private horse clients as opposed to the mustangs. Then I peer toward the barns before a hand comes down on my shoulder.

'Pass me your suitcase – I'll take it your cabin.' And Noah nods toward a small but rather adorable wooden cabin that's about a hundred yards or so from the main house, tucked neatly behind the barn. I love it. Despite Noah's arsehole-like tendencies, I'm so excited to call this place home for the next month.

Before I can answer, I hear voices coming from the main house as the front door opens and two people make their way down the porch steps.

The lady extends her hand and smiles warmly, making me feel more welcome than Noah has this entire journey. 'You must be Alice.'

I instantly recognise her voice as the woman I spoke to on the phone. 'Hey! That would be me, yes.'

'I see you've met Noah.'

I think the sideways glance I give him as he's walking my bags to the cabin tells her all she needs to know.

'Ignore everything he has to say about not needing the help. He needs it. He's going to be stubborn and maybe even a little hard work at first, but you sounded tough enough to break him down, so I figured you could handle it.'

I keep looking at him before turning back to Mrs Williams. 'A little warning would have been great, to be honest. I think I might've told him to bugger off or something along those lines when he told me I'd just be cleaning stalls for the next month.'

She struggles to stifle a laugh before turning back to who I'm assuming is her husband and saying, 'She told Noah to *bugger off*,' in the worst attempt at a British accent I've heard.

'Oh my goodness, I sure do wish I were there to hear that. There aren't many people that can put him in his place and still have him carry their bags to their cabin, that's for sure. And please, call me Brenda. This is Tom behind me. We're Noah's parents. We actually own the ranch, and while Noah may run it, I still have final say, let me tell you.'

I know without fail that I'm going to like Brenda. She's a strong, dominant woman. She takes no crap and rules the roost. We're going to get along just fine.

'Well, I'm guessing you're tried from travelling so before you go catch a little shut-eye, we're cooking dinner tonight, so make sure you're in our kitchen and at the table by six thirty. That gives you quite a few hours to catch a little sleep, settle into your cabin and maybe even have a wander around the ranch. You'll love it here. We can't wait to catch up and introduce you to life on the Orange City ranch!'

'That sounds lovely. Thank you so much, guys, for the warm welcome, and I look forward to dinner.'

I turn toward the cabin and begin to make my way over before I'm called back by Tom. 'Oh, honey, just so you know, Noah will welcome you soon, just as warmly as us. He just takes a little time. He has his guard up around people on the farm, but you work at him long enough, he'll soon come round, I promise.'

'I'll make sure I do, Mr Williams… I mean Tom!'

And with a smile and a wave, he turns on his heels to join his wife who's walking through their porch door. I love them already.

ALICE

I push open the cabin door and find myself stepping back in time. The surfaces are marked, stained. You can see the years they've spent here. The curtains tatty and old, but it's wonderful. It's everything I need. A place to rest my head and recoup after what will undoubtedly be a tiring thirty days.

Noah drops my bags by the bed and switches on some lights, then looks around, a little uncomfortable. 'It's a little shabby, but it does the job. We don't have many people stay here, as you can probably tell.

'The shower's through there. There's a bathtub too, and the TV has satellite. There's Wi-Fi that works around this area, though it cuts out at the far end there so best to stick to the front of the cabin when you need internet.'

'Thank you,' I manage, my hands clasped together in front me. I feel a little uncomfortable after our awkward car journey. He clearly doesn't want me to stay here or offer me the training I thought I'd be getting, but after the words his father spoke, I feel like I need to push a little more.

'Will I get to meet your daughter?'

'You'll hear her before you see her. She's excited to meet you.'

'I look forward to meeting her too.' I chance a smile to see if I get anything back, and to my surprise I'm not met with a grimace so there's that. I walk toward the bed and sit myself down, staring at just about anything but him – the lampshade that's covered in dust and hints back to the nineties, the rustic wooden bedside cabinet with a wonky handle and then of course those curtains again.

I watch as he steps out of the front door, but he stops and, without looking back, informs me, 'I'm truly sorry about your sister. I can't imagine what that's like. And I get that you came all the way out here, but I really don't have time to train someone so I'm afraid what you came looking for just isn't here.' And before I can answer, he's gone with the clap of a screen door.

Fuck. *We'll see about that, matey.*

On a big exhale, I take in everything around me. This cabin is truly fabulous and it's all mine for the next month – or however long I can stick it out here with him. It's small and it's clearly been around for quite some time, but bloody hell, it's so cool. It's everything I imagined it to be, from what I saw on the website and probably my own expectations.

I throw my suitcase on the bed and make a start unpacking. I feel if I unpack then I won't allow him to push me out.

Wow. Where did this new and improved me come from? I'm loving my current determination. It feels brand new. A new and improved me for all to enjoy. I'm swiftly reminded of where it came from when I take out the picture I removed from my wall and brought with me. There we are, Izzy and I, enjoying our ice lollies, being together. The last time we were together in fact, before things went downhill for her. Before I struggled to be around her without looking worried or concerned.

I start hanging up my clothes and then arrange my toiletries in the neat and compact bathroom. This is the first time I've had a bathroom all to myself. I quite like it really. No more Alex pushing my products out of the way for his.

He had more than me I'm sure.

His fake tan, his bronzer for the show ring, his cleanser, toner, moisturiser. It would have been fine had he not always finished pushing my stuff aside with a quick reminder that he had to look his best as *he* was in the spotlight, not me. I was always in his shadow.

Though it looks as if things will be no different here. Are all men like this? My father isn't. He worships my mother. They may have had struggles in their marriage, but he always adored her and now, they're as happy as they've ever been. Even in their fifties, I think they're the most romantic couple I know. Maybe it's me. Maybe I attract this kind of man?

Once all my clothes and cosmetics are laid out and I feel I've made myself at home, I flick on the TV. The American channels are awesome. The infomercials are just insane, the enthusiasm with which they sell products just incredible. We don't have anything like this in the UK. UK television and adverts, as we call them, seem so conservative in comparison.

After watching a little TV, I decide to venture outside. I feel almost nervous, wondering what it has in store for me. Noah can't be serious that he only wants me mucking out stalls. Surely he wouldn't mind me watching or playing with one or two mustangs for Christ's sake?

As I venture out, I'm met with a breeze that feels a little cooler than earlier. He wasn't wrong when he said it was getting cold. My internet skills let me down big time when I was researching the weather.

I wrap my arms around myself and begin a slow meander around what I'd call the main hub of the farm. The corral is empty, as is the arena. There are horses in the paddocks and a few grazing by the water trough. I lean over the fence, which is made out of odd bits of wood. I love how you can see the resourceful attitude on the farm, utilising what's available and making it work.

There's a dun mustang there; his black mane and points are beautiful. He looks me over and snorts. I'm clearly new to him, but given his ballsy attitude and his desire to venture toward me, I gather he's from last year's round-up.

I lean my hand over and we touch, if only briefly, but the snorting stops and he takes in my scent. He looks me over before taking another step toward me and invites me in to stroke him. He's a fan of the old ear tickle and decides he needs more than I'm currently dishing out so steps as far forward as he can without trashing the fence and leans in for more.

I'm enjoying his company when I hear a bucket crash behind me. I look over my shoulder and spot Noah, shirt off. Good Lord, he may be an arsehole but he's a bloody attractive one. His muscles look almost godlike, but then I guess I shouldn't be that surprised when he spends his days lifting bales of hay and holding on to wild mustangs for dear life. My God, I knew he was tall but with just those jeans hanging around his waist and a bare chest, he looks like a bloody man mountain. If he wasn't such a dickhead, he'd be perfect.

He looks up from the buckets and I feel myself blush. Oh blimey. This is just what I need. Going pathetic over another man. I cannot do this again. I came out here with the one goal of learning. Bettering myself. I will not get distracted by a bloody man. An arrogant one at that too.

I'm sure he's smirking at me.

Come on, Alice. You need to sort this out. You need to man up and not let a man overpower you. You are bloody empowered!

With a new confidence I never knew existed, I turn on my heels and head straight toward him. I'm not sure he was expecting it, as he immediately heads into the barn after placing the hose in a bucket.

The barn isn't as tall as it looks on the website, but it's amazing all the same. The stables are large and airy, at least fourteen feet square each. Plenty of room for the horses who are currently stabled on big straw beds munching through their hay.

Noah is in the end stable with his head down, mucking out.

'So this is where you're going to be locking me up for the next month then?'

He raises his head and looks at the wall, as if he's composing himself before he answers me.

'D'ya always ask men if they're going to be locking you up? That your thing?'

'Only if I'm pissed off after being mis-sold a training holi-day. Expect a lawsuit. If they can do it for PPI...' I laugh to myself but he looks at me blankly. 'You know, payment protection insurance? All the PPI claims?'

Still blank... *Bugger me, this is hard.*

'Don't worry, must be an English thing.'

'Must be.'

'So there aren't that many stalls. This won't take me all day. Once I've finished in here, will you grace me with your presence and show me the ropes when it comes to your training. I'd love to see what we do differently?'

'Did you not hear me earlier?'

'I sure did, but your mother told to badger the shit out of you and that you'd eventually give in. To be fair, you're looking pretty annoyed right now. I don't think it'll take much longer to get you to come round and actually provide me with the training I've paid for.'

'You paid for training?'

'Better believe it, so understand me when I say that I didn't come out here to shovel shit for you.'

'Well I guess that's a little different then.'

'Certainly is, Mr Williams.' Am I flirting with him? What the hell is going on? 'Do you need a hand with anything?'

'No, that's fine. Feel free to take a look around. The tools are over there – they'll be ready for you in the morning. I'll meet you in here after breakfast. You should probably get some sleep. We have a pretty busy day tomorrow.'

'I might get some shut-eye then before dinner. Your parents invited me over tonight.'

'They did, huh?'

'They did…' I keep his eye contact for just a few seconds before having to look away. His stare is intense, and the way he's currently leaning on the pitchfork makes me feel a little weak. I've not felt like this in years. I have no idea what's going on, but I've come out here to train, not to lust after some cowboy.

After realising I'm basically staring at my feet, I decide to make my excuses and leave. He is right after all – the new mustangs arrive tomorrow and I want to be ready to shout him down when he tries to stop me having a part of it, though by the way he just spoke, he might already be backing down.

I say a quick hello to every horse in the barn and then make my way back to the cabin. My cabin. I love it already.

I step inside and close the open window. The breeze is cool and I'm starting to feel the chill. Right now, all I want is to snuggle up under a heavy blanket and that's exactly what I'm going to do.

NOAH

*O*n my mother's orders, I'm wearing a smart shirt to dinner. I don't know why she's going to all this effort but good Lord is she. She seems pretty taken with Alice. It's the first time she's ever been happy with the female company I'm involved with. She certainly wasn't happy with Annabelle's mother.

'Daddy, what do you think? Do I look pretty to meet Alice?'

Before I can give her the answer that fills my mind before I even look at her, I spin around and see my little girl twirling. She's excited. She's excited to have someone new here. Someone who'll talk about dresses and girl things and someone who isn't her Daddy, or her grandparent.

'Honey, you look beautiful. You could wear a blanket from out of the barn and you'd still look beautiful.'

'Thank you, Daddy.' And with a squeal, she heads off toward the stairs, shouting, 'You look handsome too!'

I hear her leap down the stairs with a thud on each step and start squeaking to her grandparents about a visitor. I'd join her but I just can't get this damn collar to look right.

Damn. Why the hell am I making such a fuss right now? My palms are sweating and I'm sure my body is too. I just had a shower but I feel anything but fresh right now. What the hell is going on with me?

I'm fiddling with my tie for the hundredth time when I hear the front door shut and excited voices downstairs. I can hear Annabelle has gone up another three or four hundred decibels too.

'Ahh, fuck it.' I leave the collar open and unbutton another couple of buttons. I'm wearing the damn shirt. We're not in a restaurant. We don't need to be this formal.

I take the stairs one at a time, crouching so I fit down the small stairwell. My six-foot-three frame makes it hard to fit in just about any damn space in this cabin, but I'm used to it. It's probably why I feel more at home in the barn. Those stables are pretty big, and the ceiling height is bliss for me.

At the bottom of the stairs, I emerge straight into the kitchen where I set eyes on Alice. She's wearing a satin vest with lace inserts down the sides. One strap is sitting perfectly in place and the other one is falling down the shoulder.

'Good evening, Alice. You certainly didn't pack for the Utah winter, huh?'

Her cheeks flush red as she looks at her outfit. 'I didn't know what was appropriate to pack for evening wear.'

And just as she reaches out to adjust her strap, I notice her lack of self-confidence. Her body language changes. It's almost like she's closing up.

I reach forward and hook my finger into the strap and lift it up onto her shoulder. It feels electric. To be touching her like this. I'm feeling things I haven't felt in a long time.

I catch her eye and hold the strap in place for too long, then quickly pull my hand away, but it grazes her shoulder and collarbone. Her skin is as soft as it looks and now all I can imagine is taking that strap back down and revealing more of her skin, not hiding it.

'You look beautiful. Way too beautiful for dinner at home – well, my home… You look like you should be getting taken out to a fancy restaurant looking like that…' And as the words leave my mouth, I find myself wanting to be the one taking her. 'Maybe while you're here I can show you our only "fancy" restaurant, though I'm guessing given where you're from, it won't be that special.'

'I don't think I've ever been taken out to a fancy restaurant so sounds good to me. As long as you don't get the wrong idea. I know us Essex girls have a reputation but that doesn't ring true with me, thank you very much.' She gives me the cheekiest grin and a wink before my mom re-enters the kitchen. It floors me and makes me feel more vulnerable than I've felt in a long time.

My mom gives me the once-over. Nothing gets past that woman. I try to regain my composure after this wholly unexpected flirting, especially given the atmosphere during our ride from the airport, and roll my eyes at my mother. I take the jacket that's in Alice's hand and offer to hang it up for her, striding in front to escape my mother's scrutiny.

Annabelle skips past me and screams, 'Daddy, I love her outfit.'

I shout, 'Don't even think about it – you're too young,' over my shoulder before making my way to the coat cupboard. This night might just be a lot more interesting than I'd expected.

Since Annabelle's mother left us, I've had no time for women. That's not to say I haven't been with women. I've fucked around. I'm a man, for Christ's sake. I have needs. But I've not felt an attraction like this. It usually happens late at night, at the bar with one of the local girls that's just as bored and horny as I am after a few shots. But it's nothing like this.

No spark. No electricity. Damn. This is new and fucking exciting, but it isn't what I need right now.

After hanging the jacket up, the jacket I'm so damn glad she wasn't wearing when she came in, I make my way to the dining table.

'D'ya need any help, Ma?'

'No thank you, sweetie. Sit down with Belle and Alice and your father and I'll bring the food in.'

'Why don't you sit down and let me do it?' It comes out like a suggestion, as if she has a choice in the matter, but I'm turning her shoulders and leading her to a chair as I utter the words. She does enough. She doesn't need to wait on all of us hand and foot. Plus, I know she'll appreciate new company just as much as Annabelle.

'Pa, you can sit down too. I've got this.'

He smiles at me, adjusts his shirt and walks into the dining room too. It's been a long time since I've heard this much chatter and noise coming from that room.

And then I hear it, her laugh. God, it's almost magical. Fuck. What is this woman doing to me? I couldn't stand the thought of her being here, and when she arrived, sure I found her attractive, but I still didn't want her around. Now though? Well, now it's a different God damn story.

The sound of her laughing is doing things to me. I can help but imagine her laughing while I'm tickling her belly button, in bed, butt naked between my sheets. I've not had fun like that with a woman in years.

All it's ever been since *she* left us was fucking, just getting it out of my system. Getting what I needed. What they needed. Sure, there were women who wanted more, but I was always upfront about what I wanted, what I didn't want. And they accepted that. But now, I want to do things to her that I haven't wanted to do in a long time.

Just adjusting that strap on her barely there top, the touch of her skin. I don't need this right now. I don't need the distraction, and I especially don't need to feel like this about someone who's leaving in a month's time. Someone who probably has a partner waiting at home.

Fuck. I slam my hand down on the worktop before I'm interrupted.

'You OK? You look like you're having an argument with the wooden worktop. Did it call you an arse or something?'

I can't hide my startled look because she does her best to reassure me. 'I was just joking. Just a joke. Have I done something? Are you missing an event or something? You don't have to stay if you're just trying to be polite. Or if you need me to leave so you can go somewhere, that's fine.'

'No, no, it's nothing like that. I just remembered I forgot to do something is all.'

'Anything I can help you with?'

'No!' My head is suddenly filled with images of her *helping* me and the movement in my groin is not what I want to be happening right now.

She shoots her hands up as if I just accused her of something awful, but I guess my abrupt reaction warranted it. 'No worries, was just trying to help. Erm, I'll take some plates. Your parents were wondering where you got to so I said I'd come give you a hand.'

'No, no, it's fine. It's not you, it's me.'

'Wow, did you just break up with me and we haven't even been out on a date? I won't lie, it's never happened that quick before, ha.' She smirks at me, grabs two plates of food and makes her way into the kitchen. She's toying with me, playing with me. She can see she's made me uncomfortable, but does she know why?

Maybe she has an idea that I find her attractive? I couldn't have stared any more at her breasts within the first five minutes of meeting her, and that moment earlier, I left my hands on her too long, but she didn't push me off.

'DADDY!'

'I'm coming, sweetie.' I adjust my now uncomfortable jeans before grabbing the plates and making my way into the dining room where I find all eyes on me.

'What?'

'What the hell have you been doing in there, son? You look flustered?' My dad is eyeing me up – he looks about as confused as I feel right now.

'Nothing. I just remembered I was supposed to do something in the barn, but it's nothing that won't wait until tomorrow. Right, I hope you're hungry, Alice – we like to feed in this family.'

'Oh God, I think I'm going to be going home about a stone heavier. Everything looks delicious.'

I can't help but look at her body as she says that. At any weight, this woman would be beautiful, but I sure would like to see her eat. I can't stand a girl that toys with her food. 'You won't need to worry about what you're eating out here. You're gonna be burning a lot of calories in that barn.'

'And in that corral learning from the best of the best, right?'

'Yes, Noah, she's here to learn from you too, ya know!'

'Thank you, Ma. I've been informed of this numerous times by Alice. I will be sure to get used to my new shadow for thirty days.'

'I thought I was your shadow?' Annabelle pipes up and giggles. 'Is Alice gonna get piggybacks like me too.'

Alice coughs and almost chokes on the glass of wine she's currently holding to her lips. I smile at my beautiful daughter. Kids. They always tell it how it is and never have a single clue what they're saying. Gotta love 'em.

'I don't think your dad's going to be able to pick me up

after I eat all of this up.' And Alice makes wide eyes at Annabelle, who giggles and leans in to her new friend. It's cute watching her get excited about having someone here. I have friends, but the only time they ever come to dinner is after a hard day's work on the yard, and even then, poor Annabelle gets a bit sick and tired of listening to us talking shop.

My mother looks proud as punch, having someone new to dinner too and watching her best beef being served up. She's been marinating and working on it all day. Her smile is wide, and, as usual, she sits back waiting for everyone to fill their plate before she starts filling her own. She likes to make sure everyone has a full plate and, by default, full stomachs later.

'So, Alice, tell us about yourself. What kind of training have you done over the years? Well, during your young years.' My dad smiles sweetly and Alice covers her mouth, as if it'll help her chew faster so she can answer.

'I worked with my own two horses, both of whom were rescue cases. One is a pure-bred Clydesdale and another is a Clydesdale cross warmblood. They both had pretty rough starts and were quite volatile for a while, but we've got past that with both and I'm quite confident that we have a happy and content future ahead for the pair of them.

'I've also worked with countless horses throughout my local area, from backing youngsters to addressing behavioural issues. I've been doing it for years. It was my focus for quite a while until other things took over.'

I can't help but wonder if she's referring to her sister or something else entirely, but the curiosity inside of me won't let me wonder in silence. 'What other things would those be?'

'Erm, my boyfriend – well, ex-boyfriend – was... er still is a showjumper. His career became the focus, and I just did what I could to support him really.'

My mother has her concerned face on, which means she's going to pry further. I'd stop her but I'm too busy wondering when she split with the ex and whether he's still in the picture at all. Damn, I'm nearing forty and I'm here feeling like a schoolboy.

'Well now, that doesn't sound very fair. Are you still on good speaking terms at least, because let me tell you, it's not worth your time or your peace of mind to be on bad terms with someone.'

'Ma!'

'What? I'm just saying. It's good for, ya know, moving on and stuff.'

'Moving on?' My confusion at her *Sex and the City*-esque line has to be clear for everyone to see.

'Does she mean moving on with another boy?' Of course Annabelle has to pipe up and wind me with her ability to follow an adult conversation.

'Annabelle, no one's moving on with other boys.'

'Well I might, if I find a nice one.'

And just like that, the awkwardness I was feeling is gone and the mood becomes so much lighter.

Alice winks at Annabelle, and my little sweetie giggles. 'But in all honesty, I don't know what terms we're on. I found out he' – she glances at Annabelle – 'wasn't being very nice with someone else, so I decided to change things a little. That's when I inquired about this place and Noah's training finally! I've wanted to come here for years and now I'm finally doing it. I grabbed my things from Alex's place and boarded my flight. He's messaged but I'm way too busy now to be worrying about answering him.'

I'm blown away. I can't imagine this feisty, tenacious woman ever living in someone's shadow like that. She deserves to be front and centre in someone's life, living her own dreams, not someone else's. *Says the man who told her he didn't have time for her...*

The rest of the evening seems to go by in the blink of a slightly tipsy eye. We've all had a couple glasses of wine, even my mom, when Annabelle heads up to bed reluctantly.

She asks to have Alice tuck her in, but my mom tells her to leave our guest be. Alice winks, and just like that, it feels like she was always here. My mom yells down the stairs, a sign she's comfortable with Alice being around which warms the heart; she was never like that with Annabelle's mum.

'When I'm done putting Belle to bed, I'll be heading to bed myself. Two glasses of wine is enough for me. Are you coming, honey?'

While it sounds like a question, it's really an order and my dad recognises it as such, downing the last mouthful of his wine and giving us both a wink goodnight before quietly mouthing, 'See you both in the morning.'

As he makes his way up the stairs, I turn to Alice and hold the newly opened bottle of wine in the air.

'That wasn't open, was it?'

'It is now. Hold your glass out.' What am I doing? It's like I can't stop myself.

'Just one more. I have to be up early for work and I've heard my boss is an ass.'

I laugh as I pour the wine and try my best not to spill any, though I'm not successful. Those other two glasses have gone to my head. She wipes the wine from her jeans and takes another sip.

'Did you want to sit outside on the porch? It's nice this time of an evening. I'll get you a hoodie and blanket. It's my favourite place.'

'Sure. Sounds super American, sitting out on the porch.'

'You don't do that anywhere in the UK?'

'God no. If you sat in your porch in the UK, you'd likely be very cramped and considered extremely nosey.'

'I couldn't imagine not having a space like this. It's my favourite place to be, somewhere I can rest my mind from the day and just chill. Do you have a place like that?' I look toward her and find she's staring at me, deep into me. It's like she's reading my soul, and all I want to do is kiss her so hard it hurts.

Before I can do anything that I'll likely regret in the morning, she looks away and just watches her wine glass.

'I have a place like that. The paddock for my two horses, Jack and Alfie. I could sit there for hours. But I have to say, this place is pretty nice too. Don't have endless views like these at home. From the horizon of my field, I can see the London skyline, which is cool, but it's not this. Anyway, I think I best make my way back to the cabin. I'm absolutely knackered and I've definitely had enough wine… though I won't waste this last drop.'

I watch her throat as she gulps the last of it and think of reaching out to run my fingers down it before licking her from top to toe, but she finishes the rest of the wine quicker than I thought. Dutch courage to say goodbye without any awkwardness maybe?

'I'll walk you to your cabin.'

'Oh God, don't be silly – it's about a hundred yards! I'm safe. Unless there's any mountain lions prowling about, haha.'

Then her face drops when she sees mine.

'Wait, are there actually mountain lions out here?'

'Yeah, you get 'em. They prefer to keep themselves to themselves, but I'm not sure what they'd do if they saw a pretty little thing like you walking home alone.' And before I know it, I have hold of her upper arm and I'm staring down at her as I guide her off the front porch.

With that response, she reaches over with her other hand and holds on to me before whispering, 'To be fair, considering you're such a lightweight, I doubt you'd protect me so much as provide a distraction as you stumble and offer yourself as sacrifice.'

'Hey, whatever works to get your pretty little ass in bed safe, right?' *Shut up, Noah. Stop.* But she doesn't protest – instead, she laughs so hard she snorts.

'You know, from all the videos that I've seen of you working, never did I imagine you saying, *pretty little arse.*' And she throws her head back and laughs even harder, showing me more of that neck.

'I didn't say that; I said ASS. Say it right, English!'

We reach the porch of her cabin and I reluctantly let go of her. As she does me. She clears her throat as if she's going to say something important but reconsiders...

'Well, this is me.' And she waves to the cabin door. 'Thank you for making sure I got back safe, although I'm a little concerned with who's going to get you back safe considering the state of you.'

'The state of me? I'm perfectly fine, English.' I lean in, having to lower my head to get anywhere near her, but instead of kissing her, I resist.

'Goodnight, Alice.' I linger close to her for longer than needed, and she kisses me on the cheek goodnight. The electricity is unreal. My hand wanders up her arm, caressing it, before she puts me in my place and says a little more firmly, 'Goodnight, Noah.'

Watching her walk away feels almost painful. I could die right now with how badly I want to follow her in.

I watch as she shuts the door and then winks at me through the screen before shouting, 'See you in the morning, bright and breezy for some TRAINING!'

Fuck me, I think I've fallen in love in the space of twelve hours.

ALICE

*O*pening my eyes, I wonder if I'm hungover or just dehydrated. I don't feel sick, but my head is a bit sore. I'm also starving, though I'm not sure how after that feast. I think I'm good. What I'm not good about is last night.

Fuck. The chemistry I feel with him, despite him initially being a complete arsehole, is undeniable, but this is not what I came here for. And what's the deal with the ex-wife, Annabelle's mother? Is she still on the scene? Is she even alive? Is she just not mentioned? I couldn't see any pictures of her, and Annabelle didn't mention her either. The last thing I need is to get involved in another complicated situation. I just need to learn for the thirty days and leave – well, twenty-nine now.

First things first though – it's breakfast time. I wonder what delights Brenda will be conjuring up today? She invited me for breakfast last night as I hadn't had a chance to get to the local supermarket, so I'm rather excited.

I jump in the shower and wash off the smell of temptation, I think we can call it. I'm rinsing the conditioner from my hair when I hear Noah's voice. He's shouting to Annabelle.

I turn the shower off, fully rinsed and ready to face the day, and as I do, I hear what I assume to be the school bus doors closing and the vehicle pulling away. School buses – we don't have those in the UK. Not that I know of anyway. We either had to walk the thirty minutes or my parents would drop me and contribute to that wonderful school traffic.

I do miss my parents, but I'm feeling a renewed energy this morning. After last night, despite the all-too-close-for-comfort moments with Noah, I feel like we actually get on and this month ahead won't be so bad after all.

I wrap a towel around my hair and then one around my body after drying off roughly and head into the main room where my bed, TV and clothes drawers are. I look up to see Noah standing at the door, his hand mid-air, about to knock.

'My apologies – I didn't know you weren't decent.'

'I'm covered in a towel and I'm very decent thanks. Everything OK? Am I late? You told me to start a little later this morning, right? After you insisted I drink another glass of wine.' I smile and try my best to ease the awkwardness as opposed to adding to it.

'Yeah, we've already eaten, but there's breakfast waiting for you over at mine. I have no idea why you're showering though. The mustangs are arriving in just over an hour and you're about to get real dirty.'

It's like he hears himself say it and instantly regrets it, so I feel the need to make him feel even more embarrassed, just because he looks so bloody cute when he blushes.

'Really? Seems like you had hopes of that last night? Alas, I'm a good girl, Mr Williams, and I like to stay clean.'

I give him a wink and wait for his rebuttal, but instead, he just looks at me for a little while before quietly replying, 'We'll see about that.' And with that, he's gone.

I run to the door and watch him walk back to the main house, his jeans hugging his arse tightly and his cowboy boots doing all sorts of things to me that I never imagined.

I feel like I need a moment alone to release this tension, something I've become rather good at over the last year as attention from Alex dried up, but I glance at the clock and see that I just don't have the time to really enjoy it. Fuck.

I throw on some clothes, towel-dry my hair and then make my way to the main house, following the track left behind by Noah's huge feet on the dusty ground. I have a new spring in my step, and I'm feeling a sense of excitement that I haven't enjoyed in a long time.

Where have I been hiding?

I wave good morning to the horses across the way and skip up the front steps in my sand-coloured boots and baggy jeans. I went for my best cowgirl-style get-up. I have a sports bra and vest on ready for work, but I might also have checked that I looked good before I left the cabin – might have done anyway.

Who am I kidding? I want to look good for Noah. Christ, what am I doing?

I knock on the door and Noah answers. His gaze drags up and down my whole body, taking everything in. 'A little more "decent" now, aren't we?'

'I'm ready for a busy day. Got my work boots on, the lot.' I flash a quick glance at my River boots, which look about as worn out as my ability to resist this man. 'As soon as I finish brekky, I'll head to the barn and get a start on cleaning the stalls before the mustangs arrive so I can do that training you're super excited about. So… you gonna let me in or have I gotta eat breakfast out here?'

'Oh God, sorry, come in. Food's on the table.'

I sit down at the table and begin helping myself to bacon, eggs and hash browns. This is exactly what I need after last night. I'm halfway through munching on the bacon when Noah ventures over, grabs another slice of toast and shoves it in his mouth. He's walking as he's eating, always on the go.

Just as he reaches the door, he turns toward me and says, 'Don't worry about cleaning the stalls. I was up early so I've done it for ya. When you're finished, head to the barn and I'll show you where everything is before the mustangs arrive.'

He walks through the door and lets it shut behind him. I'm left open-mouthed at his change of heart and the dramatic change in his attitude. This playful side to him is incredibly hard to resist. I'm not sure if that's a good thing or a bad thing, but what I do know is I like him way more than I should do right now.

'Morning, Alice. Did you sleep well?' I'm brought out of my trance or, rather, my obsessive staring by Brenda.

'I slept beautifully, thank you so much. And thank you for this amazing breakfast. It's delicious. Just what I needed. I'm definitely going home a stone heavier, at the very least, after this month.'

'Oh be quiet. You're a tiny thing. Besides, you can afford to eat whatever you want. Going by the amount of work in front of you, I think you're gonna need it. Noah's already cleaned the barn, ya know?' And she smiles as me, knowing what it means to me that I haven't been sent to the barn for the day – instead I have a day ahead of working with real wild mustangs. I couldn't be more excited if I'd won the lottery right now.

I quickly finish up my breakfast, making sure to enjoy every single bite before heading out of the Williams' front door and straight to the barn. It's literally a hop, skip and jump to get there, and when I do, Noah's there looking more at home than ever.

'I see Annabelle got the school bus this morning. It's cool. I wish we had those in the UK.'

'You don't have school buses?'

'No, we have to walk, or if the school's too far, parents drive you. You can get public transport of course, but where I am, there are no dedicated school buses.'

'It's so different in the UK.'

'Well, yeah. Very different.'

'So, you were saying last night, you came here because you left a guy?'

'Wow, straight in there with the big questions, ha!' I wander over to the bucket that's sitting under a running tap, ready to overfill and turn the water off. I pick the bucket up and look at him. 'Which stable is this going in?'

He almost jumps to attention. 'Ahh, right over in this one.' And he opens the door and throws a hand in the direction of a tyre that I'm to sit the bucket in.

'Umm… so, the boyfriend.'

'Is he still your boyfriend?'

'No, not at all.' I'm perched on a stool outside one of the stables, staring down at my feet. As I study the scuffed toes on my boots, I realise I haven't really spoken about this with anyone. People know what happened – well, some do anyway – but they don't know the details.

'I found out, through someone who's always pursued him, that he was actually living a double life, shagging some other woman. A better one of course. More beautiful, more talented, blah blah. Turns out he was using me. I was always looking after his horses, so he never had to fork out for a groom, and I trained them. I was always there. Put my career on hold for him. Did everything for him, so I think he was reluctant to lose me and all that came with me. He has a few hot-tempered showjumpers who, without the right training, would make life difficult for him. I used to train them, ya know, keep them in his good books.'

I laugh at what I'm saying because it's only now that I realise. 'You know, it's only just occurred to me that she wasn't more talented than I am. If she was so good, he'd have been happy to let her take my place instead of lying and treating me like a piece of shit. I'm good at what I do. That's why he did it. He's calculated. Narcissistic. A real piece of fucking shit, and I won't be treated like that anymore. I'm worth more than that, and I won't settle for anything less.'

By the time I finish my rant, I'm standing tall, shoulders broad. I need to give myself more talks like this. Pep myself up. Make myself realise what I'm worth.

'So what about you, Noah? Why are you a single Pringle?'

He looks caught out. I'm guessing these are the sort of questions I shouldn't be asking, but I'm curious. All I thought about last night, this morning and right now is how much I want to taste those lips, and while I didn't come out here to get involved with someone, I can't help but wonder what's going on.

He's a beautiful man. Tall, muscular and dark. He works with horses and has a wonderful family. I don't understand why he's single.

'Single Pringle? Is that what they call it now? Who said I'm single?'

'Oh, I'm sorry, I just thought…'

'No, I'm messing. I am. But I don't really have time to be with someone so I guess I don't see myself as single.'

'What do you see yourself as then?'

'Not looking?' Then he corrects himself. 'Not looking for something serious anyway. I think I'd end up hurting whoever I tried to be in a relationship with. Annabelle comes first and always will. There's nothing that will ever change that, and working the farm takes up a lot of my time too. I just don't see how I can change that.'

'Is that why Annabelle's mum isn't around?'

'That's none of your business.' And just like that, he shuts me down and immediately closes himself off.

'I'm sorry, I didn't mean to overstep the mark. You asked me about my ex – I figured I could do the same with you.'

'Well you can't. That's none of your business, and it needs to stay that way.'

While I'm incredible embarrassed and apologetic, the anger building inside of me is unexpected. Being recently treated like shit by a man has left a bitter taste in my mouth and I'm struggling to remain polite, especially when I feel like I've not done much wrong but ask about his ex, much like he did me.

'I'm going to get the corral ready. They'll be here soon. We don't need to be wasting time in here.'

And we're right back to where we were when we first met. God, this man is infuriating.

I hate myself. I don't know what I want, and I don't know what I should be doing right now, with these feelings, with the attraction I'm feeling, but it's sure as hell not what I just did.

Why the hell did I talk to her like that? There was absolutely no need whatsoever, but the thought of her finding out why Annabelle's mother isn't around makes me feel sick. I've never cared. Everyone in this town knows and it's never bothered me, but I don't want her to know. I can't have her know what sort of guy I really am, deep down.

She flew all the way over here because she's followed my career, thinks I'm some big-shot horse trainer, and while I won't deny I'm good at what I do, I can't pretend I'm a good guy behind the scenes. Last night was unreal, but if today has shown me anything, it's that nothing can happen. No good can come of this. She'll find out the sort of guy I am and run a mile. I can't get involved here, with her. I can't do that to Annabelle – and, more importantly, with the way I'm feeling right now, I can't do that me. I've not loved a woman since

Annabelle's mom and won't go down that road again. When I love, I love hard, and I can't fall for someone who doesn't know what I'm really like or worse still, is going to be leaving in a little under a month.

No, she can't find out what I did.

The only way to ensure that is to keep her at a distance, so that's what I'm going to have to do. I'm going to have to be a man about it and stop thinking with my dick, or my heart, or whatever the hell is going on here and just stop.

I look up to see if she's still in the barn with me. It's been pretty quiet since our last conversation. After I sorted out the corral, I came back to show her where the hay and feeds are – all straight feeds here compared to her mixes and whatever else she seems to feed in the UK. We like to keep it simple. It definitely broke the ice a little, as she was fascinated at how simple we keep it. Indeed, she seems to prefer keeping the ingredients basic compared to the endless list of additives and preservatives in her 'whole feeds'.

We keep things nice and easy with oats – barely any unless they need fattening up – and basic fibre pellet. They have a chaff too to make it more palatable and slow them down when they're eating, but generally speaking, the mustangs that come in don't tend to eat too much. They graze and we give them hay, but with the wild ones, we try to keep it super simple, only introducing hard feed if we absolutely have to, and even then it's pretty minimal.

I can hear the sound of the float in the background and look up. I tap her on the shoulder – we're still only using words if we absolutely have to – and the electricity that bolts through me could very well knock me off my feet. I'm a big guy – people comment on it often – and it takes an awful lot to make me feel uncomfortable or out of sorts, but right now, I'm feeling that bad, and it's down to this pretty little thing here with the attitude of a wild mustang mare. Damn, I wish things were so different right now.

She looks up at me then immediately looks away when she catches my eye, until I point toward the barn door and the dust kicking up from the tyres of the huge float that's now parking outside.

'They're here…'

'Oh my God. Oh my God! The mustangs are here? They're going to be unloaded now? Are you kidding me?'

The joy and anticipation on her face makes me break into the biggest smile, which in turn makes her blush. That flush that creeps across her cheeks and round her eyes does things to me. The fact that I want to make her blush for other reasons but can't is causing me a whole world of pain right now so that's going to have to do. I'll just have to settle for some pretty wicked thoughts when I'm on my own later tonight.

I put my hand on her side because it feels so fucking natural and smile even harder at her blushing. 'Come on – don't you wanna meet 'em? There are thirty-five apparently, though sometimes the numbers change. So don't be disappointed if we're missing a few.'

'Just to see one would make me bloody orgasmic— Oh!'

Her hand goes straight to her mouth as if the word escaped without her realising, and boy, I can't let it go.

'I didn't mean that. What I meant was—'

'Well damn, if just seeing a wild mustang would do that to you, I wonder what a good man would do?' I literally can't help myself where she's concerned.

That flush moves down her neck and onto her chest, my gaze following suit, and out of the corner of my eye, I see her cock a hip.

'Oh now you want to play? Now you want to flirt and be

nice? Fuck me, Noah, you're seriously hard work. You blow hot and cold more that anyone I think I've ever met.'

'We're flirting, are we?'

'We were until you decided to be a fucking dick.'

'A dick? Well fuck me, woman. I've never had a single barn hand call me a dick in the thirty-something years I've been on this farm. You sure are full of yourself.'

'You sure are full of yourself for someone who doesn't have a fucking clue how to be around a woman.'

Ouch. Right in the gut. That one was a low blow, but I can't say that she's wrong. She's read me like an open book, but that doesn't mean I won't try to deny it.

'Hey. I know exactly how to handle myself around a woman, and I'd be more than happy to show you. I'm just trying to remain professional for the sake of your training. Now quit your talking and let's get to these mustangs, shall we?'

Have I technically just told her I'd like to make a move on her? I think I have. So much for staying away from her.

As the flush in her cheeks begins to fade, her face instead takes on an expression of awe. It's just as endearing. She's listening to the guys in the float and taking a peek through the open slats.

She looks back at me like a kid on Christmas morning. 'There are some real young ones in there – like six-months-old young.'

'God damn, really?'

'Why is that a bad thing?'

'Because you can't work a youngster. We can handle them and get them easy on the end of a rope, but you can't work them, as you'll know, and that makes them harder to find homes for. That just makes them expensive for me to keep, when really I only do this to help out the mustang itself. I have enough young mouths to feed – I don't need any more.'

'Oh, I didn't even realise that this costs you.'

'Sure does. We take on a set amount each year. Train and then rehome. I don't get paid to take them, but I do get to make a little money back when I rehome them. That being said, it barely covers the cost to keep them and get them working. I wish money didn't have to come into it, but it does. Though I guess that's just the world we live in.'

'I'd be happy to chip in if that helps? I can buy some food and stuff. Pay for their hooves to be done. Whatever helps?'

My heart swells at her offer. She really just wants the best for these horses, and I can't tell you how wonderful it is to see. I've never met someone as in love with this animal as I am, I don't think. All too many that work with these guys are in it for the money or to win some fancy title for training them in so many days. I just want to help them remain a part of our lives, whether that's as domesticated pets or, better still, running free, where they really belong.

'I think you've already paid enough to get training from this amazing trainer, haven't ya?'

'Well, I wouldn't say he's amazing. He's hot, but he's a seriously arrogant arsehole, so I'm actually looking forward to spending more time with the horses in all honesty.'

'It's a shame she's leaving in a month, coz I have it on good authority that this trainer wouldn't mind getting to know her better.'

'Who says we can't have a little fun? Rebounds are meant to be all the rage, you know?'

I've spent less than twenty-four hours in the company of this woman and with one line, just a smattering of words, she's made me feel like I won the lottery. She couldn't have made it any clearer that she's only looking for fun. We can have *fun* and she needn't know about my past, and then when it's done, it's done. If I know that's what it is, I can stick to those terms. Sure, I think it'll sting when she leaves, but it's this or nothing, and right now, nothing isn't an option, because I'm sure as shit not going to be able to keep my hands off her if the last few hours has been any kind of indicator.

'Let's crack on with these mustangs, shall we then? I'm excited to get them out.'

And just like that she reverts back to her awed state, wanting to catch a glimpse of these magnificent beasts as much as I do. Though if I'm being honest with myself, I want to catch a glimpse of her more.

We spend the next hour unloading the mustangs into four separate corrals round the back of the house. There were only twenty-five in total, five of which were youngsters barely older than six or seven months. Alice is in love with them already, naming them all and checking out their confirmation and deciding their future disciplines. I could watch her all day. How enamoured she is with these animals is beautiful to see, but I need to remind myself that if anything's going to happen right now, it's temporary and just a bit of fun. She even used the word rebound. She couldn't make it any clearer if she tried, but right now, I'm not complaining.

'Alice, I know you want to stay here all day and make friends with these guys, but I think we're going to have to run into town. You can come and check out the local feed if you want? It's not too far a journey.'

'Oh yeah, I'd love to. I want to see what your places are like. A little different to my local saddlery I bet?'

'No doubt.' I chuckle at her excitement to see the feed store, a rundown old place managed by Jimmy and June Earl. They're wonderful people, but they're getting on a bit now and I know it's a struggle for them. But like all old folk around there, they refuse to give up to 'sink into retirement' as they call it.

We head to the truck, and the thought of being alone with this woman in such a small space makes me all kinds of nervous. I need to keep my hands to myself and wait for her to make a move. She's the one on the 'rebound' as she put it, and now I don't think that word will ever leave my head. Is this a good thing or a bad thing? I'm not entirely sure...

ALICE

*D*id I actually just suggest a fling with the man I've flown thousands of miles to train under? What the fuck has got into me? I can't believe how brazen I'm being, but he just seems to bring it out in me.

Though, if I'm being honest, is that really so bad? We could have fun on top of our training while I'm here. No one has to get hurt. I go home in a month. It doesn't need to be serious. I could just have the fun I've been missing out on for the last however many years. God only knows, my sister would be proud of me for letting loose.

My only concern is that he now assumers I'm some massive slag who jumps the bones of any bloke that gives her a wink. Having said that, I leave in a month anyway, so in all honesty, he can think what he wants.

I like this new me. A me that goes after what she wants, that throws caution to the wind and screws (literally) the men she wants, as opposed to being screwed over myself.

I fell in love with just about every one of those mustangs that came off the trailer. The young ones especially I'm just smitten with, but there's one chestnut – a spunky stallion

55

with a backside that just looks like one awesome engine. His neck is short and thick, and his trunk is as thick as the rest of him, but he's got some fantastic-looking legs. He's compact and muscular, yet looks seriously athletic. He's a lot smaller than I'm used to, owning two heavy horses, but he looks like a little powerhouse. I named him Steve. I love completely human names for horses, and he looked like a total Steve. Steven if he was being a git, which he looked like he'd be often.

I'm currently sitting next to Noah in his truck. He says there's someone I need to meet on the way into town. I'm not sure who he means. Though as we turn left onto a dusty track that immediately meets a barbed-wire fence, I realise who he's referring to. We're met by the gentle whinny of a black mustang, one that it would seem knows Noah and his truck all too well.

I look toward Noah and see a wide smile across his face. The black mustang is flanked by two chestnut mares who follow dutifully behind him, allowing him to lead the way.

As I slide out of the truck's passenger seat, Noah introduces me. 'So this is Onyx. Onyx and his two girls came to me last year and they became friendly with me pretty quickly. The only trouble is, they're pretty friendly with me and Annabelle but no one else.'

'Hmmm, so if they like me, that's like giving me the seal of approval, right?'

'Well I guess so. But we won't know until we see, right?'

'I suddenly feel more nervous meeting these guys than I ever have meeting anyone else.' I needn't be nervous thankfully. As I pop my hand over the barbed wire, Onyx sniffs me and comes closer. As do 'the girls', which I'm equally grateful for.

'Seems like they like ya. They're a good judge of character

these guys, ya know. So I'm pretty impressed that they've given you the once-over and seem unperturbed.'

'Oh wow, thanks very much. I can't say I'm too surprised though. Animals have a great idea of people. My parents' dog hated Alex.'

'But you always ignored the dog's instincts?'

'For some strange reason, yes. Don't think I would now.'

I look away from the black mustang to Noah and find him analysing me. It feels as though he's undressing me with his eyes. I wonder if he's running what I said through his mind already? I wouldn't be surprised given the gaze that's sweeping from my ankles to the top of my head right now. The tension is unreal, and all I want to do is pounce on him, but I won't. The way I spoke this morning was already pretty outrageous for me. I think it's best I leave it at that for today.

I turn on my heels and make my way to the truck, knowing his gaze is following me, then look back over my shoulder to confirm my thoughts before opening the passenger door.

'Now I've got their approval, are we grabbing that foal feed or what?'

I close the door feeling almost triumphant and way too excited for my own good.

NOAH

*T*he whole journey into town was spent talking about anything and everything, the conversation flowing far easier than I've ever experienced with a woman. Our flirting is getting more intense by the moment, and I can only thank the heavens above when we reach the feed store. Any longer alone in the car and I think I might have had to pull over and do things that I wouldn't normally dream of doing to a woman I barely know.

Her face is once again a picture. She's never seen an American-style feed store and she's making it known, her eyes wide, her mouth dragging on the floor.

I open the door for her and watch her walk in, aghast.

'Wow. Check out this place. Oh my goodness. Look at these halters. Wow, we don't have anything like this back home. Oh my God, look these! Look at the sequins. Wooooowwwwww.'

The last wow was strung out as some cowboy boots caught her eye.

'A little different to your river boots, right?'

'Just a bit. These are amazing!' And she twirls a pair of

black-and-grey cowboy boots in her hands. 'I can't believe I'm holding a pair of real-life cowboy boots. You know, not cowboy-*looking* boots but actual cowboy boots from the States. They're amazing.'

'You going to try them on or what?'

'Oh God no. No. I wouldn't wear them back home so seems a waste to buy them for the short time I'm here. Besides, we've got more important things to grab while we're here, right? Where's the foal feed?'

'That's a damn shame. You in those boots…'

'And nothing else right?'

I almost choke at the thought and find myself getting a little hot under the collar without being able to do a damn thing. God, this woman is good.

Grabbing a few bags of foal pellets, we make our way back to the truck and I find her still searching the town and its shops with her gaze.

'We haven't got to be back for a little while. The horses need to settle in, and they've got hay in their corrals. Annabelle won't be back from school for another few hours. I could always show you the town. We could grab a bite to eat if you like?'

'Sounds like a plan, Stan!'

'Stan?'

'Yeah, it rhymes. Just go with it, Noah.' And she takes my arm and leads me in the direction of town.

We grab lunch, we visit stores and then we even have a quick drink (mine non-alcoholic) in one of the local bars. It's like we've been together for an eternity and are getting to find out about each other all over again.

We finally decide it's a good time to return to the truck. Alice is looking a little tipsy, but I can't deny I love it. She's letting loose even more than she usually does, and I can't help but find it increasingly attractive. Her guard is completely down, even when talking about Alex, and her confidence is at full charge. She might be the most attractive woman I've ever come across in my life.

Walking back to the truck, Alice has her hand on my arm as if we're together. If any other woman had done this, I'd have shaken her off within seconds, but with Alice, I'm enjoying it too much.

'Well, well, well, Noah, who's this?'

I recognise her instantly, her voice grating on me. It's an ex – well, an ex-fling who never took me at my word when I said I wasn't looking for anything more than some fun.

'Helen. I hope you're well? This is Alice. She's staying with us for the next month carrying out some training.'

Alice has straightened up and immediately removed her hand from my arm. She feels uncomfortable, and I want that to stop straight away so I take her hand back and place it straight on my arm.

She looks at me in confusion, but I give her a wink and squeeze her hand to reassure her that all's well.

'Wow, you certainly don't wait around. Didn't you just have little Lucy in your bed last week? And now... Alice is it?'

'Excuse me? I'm in no one's bed, thank you very much – not that it's any of your business.'

'Oh pardon me. It's just that where we're from, we don't go walking round with our hands over gentlemen if we aren't involved. Though saying that, with Noah's track record, he's had hands all over him from just about every single woman in this town so I'm not surprised. He's pretty hard to resist at times. I should know.'

Helen and I were high-school sweethearts, but when we left school, we grew apart, and I met Annabelle's mother. She took it pretty hard, and I made it worse by going back to her when Annabelle's mother left. Despite telling her over and over again that I didn't want anything more than a little fun, she chased and chased, even going as far as turning up at my mother's house and introducing herself to Annabelle as *Daddy's new friend*.

I was furious. I threw her out and demanded she stay away from there on out, but ever since, she's tried her hardest to get back into my good books. She's always been bitchy to women she sees me with, and I guess Alice is no exception. Thankfully, she hasn't met a woman quite as sharp tongued as Alice so I have a feeling this is going to be fun.

'Maybe he's bored of them and needs a little something more exciting then, you know, to keep his attention. Now, why don't you run along and let us get back to what we were doing… having a pleasant time.' And with that, she takes my arm and drags me back to the truck.

'Who is that bitch?' she asked once we were out of earshot.

'Wow, you get a mouth on you when you've had a drink.'

'Oh, Noah, I have a mouth on me without a drop of alcohol, but I'm pretty sure you're aware of that.'

'Oh I certainly am…'

We spend the rest of our day enjoying the mustangs. We make notes of how many mares, how many young stallions and how many foals we have. We sex the foals and then start looking at their sizes, their soundness and their response to humans, and along the way, Alice names each and every one of them. The day seems to whizz by in a flash, and I find myself wishing that it wouldn't. I know the old saying 'time flies when you're having fun', but boy I wish it wouldn't. I want time to slow down.

Before I know what's happened, her first day is almost over and we're no longer alone as Annabelle and my mother both join us in the barn. Instead of dealing with the tension that's surrounded us both all day, we're being told about dinner tonight as well as the local mean girl at school and how she got her comeuppance in the dinner hall.

Alice looks enthralled throughout Annabelle's entire story, and if I'm not mistaken, genuinely too. Seeing them together makes me pine for something that will never be, and without being able to do anything about it, I'm sad. I'm sad for a future I feel Annabelle will never have. I'll likely never leave this ranch, and as a result, I'll never find that person she needs in her life, something she's missing so badly – a mother figure. Alice is the first woman in a long time who's made me think of anything like that and someone that, deep down, I could picture that with, yet she's leaving so soon.

I worry this is going to make Annabelle ask questions or even worse still, want something she simply can't have.

As we finish off the horses for the evening – with Annabelle's help of course – my mother lets us all know that dinner will be served at 7 p.m. sharp. Tonight we're having shepherd's pie, an English dish she's giving a whirl. I can tell she loves having a guest to cook for.

'Oh wow, Brenda, I'm very excited to try it – I'm sure it'll be delicious.'

'Oh thank you, dear. You make sure you go wash up now. Don't be late. Noah can finish off in here.' And she gives me the nod to tell me to back her up.

'I can indeed. There isn't much to do, so you go ahead and clean up.'

Alice puts the bucket she's carrying in the end stable before wrapping her arms around herself, giving me a sweet smile and running out of the barn to her cabin. When she came to the States, she didn't have a clue that the weather would be anything but boiling hot and she's just spent most of the day cold. Her cheeks are a little flushed, and while I'd like to think that's a lingering effect of the alcohol, I know better. I'm pretty sure she's just as excited as I am about the after-dinner meet that I've been alluding to all day. After the rebound remark, I haven't been able to keep my thoughts to myself, and she's responded to every single thing I've said with pure excitement and lust. What I would've given to have thrown her down in the barn, but by the time we got back, it was just too damn close to deliveries and Annabelle coming home for me to do anything about my desires.

I tell Annabelle to make her way inside and start washing up, ready for dinner, and fill the last bucket of water. The whole time I'm thinking of an excuse to make my way over to her cabin and then it hits me – the coat.

I run inside and find my old high-school soccer jacket. *Perfect.* This will do it. I grab it and run downstairs to the kitchen, finding my mother, who's suddenly eyeing up the literal nostalgia hanging in my hand.

'What have you got there, son? I haven't seen that in years.'

'Alice is cold. She didn't bring a coat. I figured this would work. Could keep her warm and save her spending money on a coat that she probably won't wear after she leaves.'

'Hmmmm.'

'What do you mean hmmmm?'

'I just mean hmmmm.'

'Oh God damn, Mom. I'm just loaning the girl a coat.'

'Your prized football jacket. You're going to let her work the horses in your football jacket?'

'It doesn't mean anything. It's the only one I have that will fit her.'

'Suit yourself, son.'

I leave before any further questioning, but I can't escape her scrutiny. She knows me better than I like to admit, and right now, she has every idea about what I'm thinking right now.

She's gone in under a month. Don't forget that, I have to remind myself before I start having too much fun here. I really need to make myself see that this can't be any more than what it's going to be. A fling. A fun fucking fling but a fling nonetheless. But right now, I'd take anything just to touch her.

I rap my hand on her screen door and, through the smokey coloured screen, see her coming out of the bathroom with a towel wrapped around her. *Fuck.*

She opens the screen door and steps back, inviting me in.

'I brought you a jacket. You've been cold all day and I figure we've got some real work to do tomorrow so I don't want you to be cold. This should keep you warm.'

'Is this an American football jacket?'

'Well it's not British.'

'Oh you're a sarcastic arsehole when you want to be, aren't you?'

'Yes, miss, I am.'

'Are you coming in or what?'

My mouth goes dry and I suddenly feel nervous. I've never been nervous around women, but this time it feels different. This time, I'm not just getting my end away. This time, it feels more about pleasing her than it does pleasing me. The thought of touching her is too exciting to contain, and I want to make sure this is perfect in every way, but at the same time, I just want to get that towel off.

I can see her cheeks are still flushed – the effects of the alcohol haven't worn off completely. She's more brazen than she's been before, but after our discussion about having fun, I know what the score is. She's missed out on a lot following this guy Alex around, and now she wants to be in control. Now she wants to have the fun she thinks she should have been having these last few years, and God knows I want the same. I want her to be in control, as much as I may try to fight it.

'So this is what all the cheerleaders coveted at school, right?' She holds the jacket in her hands and gives it the once-over, eyeing it up before letting her gaze rip through me, from the floor to the ceiling. Her mind is clearly tossing and turning, trying to think of something to say or questioning what to do or maybe even deciding whether her ideas are good ones. And then her face changes.

She looks at me, determined and filled with lust, then her hand slowly reaches up and grabs the piece of towel that's tucked neatly under her arm. She pulls it out, and before I can say anything, the towel falls to the floor, showing me her body in all its glory.

I step back and slide my hand out of the screen door and bring the outside front door to a close. We lose a little light, but there's still enough for me to see her put my football jacket on. Her hair is soaking wet and gets flicked out from underneath the collar to sit on top. The jacket falls down and covers her nipples and her hips. It's a little big but loose enough in front for me to still see her beautiful body in all its glory. I couldn't be any happier right now if I tried.

'Well what do you think? Does it look good on me or what?'

'Fuck…' is all I manage to say. Her body is doing things to me that I've never experienced before, and I can't hold back anymore.

I reach out and run my knuckle from her belly button up her stomach and graze her breasts. She inhales – sharply. I reach inside the jacket and graze my finger across her nipple. It's hard and clearly reacting to my touch, as is she. She's as turned on as I am.

I move closer and bring my other hand up to her face, cupping her jaw. My thumb slides into her mouth, and as soon as she sucks on it, I feel any ounce of the gentleman inside me leave. He's gone and now it's just me, a hungry asshole of a man with a beautiful woman in front of me. But she's had a drink. Is this taking advantage? Will she regret this in the morning?

'You're drunk.'

As she reaches for my belt, pulling me even closer, she reassures me. 'I'm not drunk. I wasn't even tipsy at lunch, and if you still think that alcohol has any effect on me then we might need to have a chat about booze. Right now, I'm a horny single woman who's enjoying an attractive man touching her naked body and would like to do a little more about it. Is that OK?'

'Yes, miss.' And with that, I accept my permission and take the woman in front of me, throwing the jacket to the floor before grabbing her jaw with both hands and kissing her so hard I could have very well knocked her over.

She responds with just as much hunger, just as much force, our tongues colliding in a clash of haste and desire, wanting to be as close as possible. She's tearing at my sweaty vest, trying her best to rip it off and over my head but not wanting to break our kiss, not for one second.

I pull away and lift it off, and as I do, she reaches for my belt, almost wrenching it open. As she pulls the buckle away and undoes the top button, she glances up to find me looking down at her beautiful, hungry face. Her eyes are hooded and filled with lust.

Her head arches back a little as I squeeze her nipple, watching her unzip my jeans, my dick bursting to escape. I want her and I want her now, but I'm letting her do this at her pace, in her own time.

She unzips my jeans then reaches inside the now obvious bulge that's there and grabs my shaft. I hiss as she touches me and grab her whole breast, pulling her in closer with my other hand. But as I do, she drops to her knees and pulls my cock out. It bursts out of my pants and meets her face. Her eyes wide, she licks her lips and looks up at me as she takes me whole in her mouth.

The tip of my now dripping cock hits the back of her throat, and I hear her almost gag. I run my hand through her hair then place it at the back of her head. The restraint it's currently taking not to fuck her face is unreal and quite frankly not something I thought I had in me. I want her so badly right now. I want to throw her down and fuck her brains out, but this isn't just about me – this is about her. After her last relationship, she seems as burnt as I am, so I want this to be about her too.

She licks and sucks my cock, guiding her own mouth with her hands as she runs it up and down my shaft, but I pull back and she leaps up – her confidence gone in a dash and her face full of worry. 'What? What's wrong? Did I hurt you?'

'No, baby, you didn't hurt me. You're just too good at that. You keep going and this is going to be over very quickly.'

'Oh,' she sighs as a satisfied smile creeps across her face.

'This isn't all about me, ya know,' I remind her as I trace my hand down the side of her body, brushing her hip before I slide it round the back to her ass.

She gasps as I squeeze her ass so hard I'm pretty sure it'll leave a mark – and no doubt a little bruise for later – then slide my other hand around, and with both on each ass cheek, I lift her up and bring her face to my eye level, kissing her as I do. Our tongues meet, and she tastes like citrus. Her hair smells of coconut. My senses are flooded, my cock aching to be inside her as she wraps her legs around my waist.

I walk forward, almost blind until we reach the bed, then, wrapping one arm around her waist, I free up the other and guide myself down to the bed where I gently lay her down. I trail kisses down her neck and over each breast, licking and sucking her nipples as I do. She has a hand in her hair and another sliding between her legs as she starts to pleasure herself.

What the fuck is she doing? Doesn't she know that's my fun?

I grab hold of her hand and put one of her fingers, now covered in her own wetness, into her mouth. 'Taste that. See how good you taste?'

'How do you know?'

'I know you're going to taste amazing, now stop taking that away from me. When we're together, you don't touch yourself – I touch you. I please you. I make you come so hard you fucking scream these cabin walls down. Understood?'

'Yes, sir.' Her words are lust filled as she lays her head back, knowing exactly where I'm going.

I slide my tongue along her lower stomach and find her mound. She's wet and wanting. I lick and suck as I find her clit and suddenly feel sharp nails in the back of my head. Fuck, this is unreal. She tastes better than I could have ever imagined.

She bucks, letting me know I've found that sweet spot, and it's not long before her breaths are getting short and I can feel her getting wetter and wetter. I slide a finger inside her as I nibble and suck her clit, and that seems to be her undoing, her thighs squeezing around me.

I reach up and grab her breasts as she unfolds before placing my hand over her mouth, trying to keep her silent before someone hears. The cabin is way too close to my parents' house for her to let herself go much, but I already plan to fuck her a little further away from home next time so I can let her go as wild as she needs.

She's lying back, eyes closed, catching her breath when I

kick her legs open. She looks up at me and pulls a condom from her night stand. I suddenly realise that's what she was doing when she left me in the bar earlier. Smart girl knows what she wants.

She rips open the wrapper and starts to sit up, pushing me to standing as she does. I'm tall enough that when she's sitting on the bed, my dick isn't too far from her eye level. She tilts her head and takes me in her mouth again, only this time she works me hard. *Fuck.* I can't keep this up for much longer, not if I'm gonna fuck her too. God, this is too much. I pull her off me.

'Honey, if you want me to fuck you, you're gonna have to ease up on that there.'

I lay her down, knowing full well I'm not going to last much longer. She turns me on in ways I never imagined and that's going to be my undoing very soon, but right now, I need to be inside of her pussy, not her mouth.

I lean into her, kissing her gently this time, knowing she's worn out and spent, but I fully intend to make her come all over again. Then I push her back and put a little more of my weight onto her, pushing her legs apart with my knees as I go. My cock is at her opening, and just the tip touching her is killing me.

'God, you're beautiful. You have no idea how much you're turning me on right now.'

'If it's anything close to how you're making me feel then I have a pretty good idea.'

'I'm gonna fuck you so hard right now, but, honey, I warn ya, what you were doing with that pretty little mouth of yours has come close to tipping me over the edge one too many times.'

Her hands reach around and grab my ass, pulling me in, and fuck me, if I didn't have to worry about people hearing, I think I'd likely scream myself. God damn this feels good.

I pull away from her wet and wanting mouth and look up, lifting my torso. I want her to come again, but if I fuck her for any length of time, she's going to be my undoing first. I want her to come while I'm inside of her so I slowly start to massage her clit once more.

She's still sensitive from earlier and bucks at my touch, her back arching and making her breasts bounce. I find her sweet spot once more, and as I slowly thrust in and out of her, I massage harder, faster, seeing her cheeks flush again and her back arch further. She reaches out to me, scratching at my arms, and tells me, 'I'm going to come again.'

I feel her tighten around my shaft and start to pump faster, harder, keeping my rhythm with my finger. As she comes undone, I feel her pulse around me, and it's enough to make me come too.

Both of us fall to the bed in a state of sheer exhaustion and satisfaction, and just stare at the ceiling. I wonder what the fuck has just happened and what this means for the next month. I wish I could understand what's going through her brain, I really do.

How is it that things can feel so incredibly right while you're having sex and immediately after, I'm wondering whether I've just fucked up completely, because the way I'm feeling right now, I already don't want her to leave when her training's up.

'Well I'm pretty sure I'm going to need another shower now. What's the time?'

I look over at the clock and see that it's 6.50 p.m. 'Oh shit – dinner's in ten minutes. Fuck.'

She starts laughing as she's wrapping the sheet around herself.

'What are you doing?'

'Er, I'm covering my modesty!'

'Honey, I've just been inside you. I've just licked you to

heaven and back and then fucked you senseless. I've just watched you suck my cock so hard I could have come in your mouth in seconds. You don't need to cover up that beautiful body of yours to walk to the shower. Now put the sheet down and give me one last little look before I have to leave to go home and shower myself.'

With that, she drops the sheet and saunters to the shower, giving me that cheeky grin over her shoulder as she does. As much as I'd love to join her, I know there's going to be a lot of talk back at the house about where I got to so I quickly dress and make my way back as I hear her turn on the shower.

My life just got a whole lot more interesting than I thought it was going to be this month.

ALICE

inner last night was interesting. I couldn't help but blush every time Noah talked to me, which was a lot. I thought he was going to 'walk me home' which was code for 'come fuck my brains out and make me scream while everyone's sleeping' but Annabelle called him just as we were discussing a 'nightcap' so he had to go. I know he wanted to though, which was enough for me. I might have had to satisfy myself a little, which wasn't half as enjoyable as if he'd been doing it, but he's made me feel sex starved twenty-four-seven.

I've never experienced sex like that before. Alex was OK. And yes I did come sometimes, but fuck me, I've never come twice in one session. Nor have I ever come that hard before. I've never had someone so intent on pleasing me either. With Alex, if I came, it always felt more like a happy accident as opposed to an intention.

We spend the next day working with the colts. We muck out the barn together, to get all twenty stalls done quickly, and then make our way to the mustangs. I sit and watch him as he explains his process. How he analyses a horse and what he looks for. I'm honestly amazed at how he turns on his trainer way of thinking. It's like last night never happened – he's that immersed in it. It's beautiful to watch him at work, making them move, taking control of their feet and getting them to understand that he isn't a threat but an ally, someone to partner up with. By the end of the day, he's halter broke three and I've witnessed every single minute of it, with running commentary at all times. It's truly magnificent to watch.

Just as I'm starting to feel a little starved of attention however, he asks me if I want to go see the black gelding again, on our way into town. We need some more rope for the halters, and in his words, 'It's pretty private up there,'

The excitement racing through me right now is too much to describe. Before I can answer, he's taken my hand and led me to the truck, which is noticeably empty in the back as opposed to being filled with junk as it was yesterday. Today, there's nothing but blankets in there.

Oh God, I'm getting wet at the thought of what he's going to do to me.

I slide into the truck and shut the door, looking at him as he puts himself in the driver's seat.

'My my, you're looking pretty damn excited to go see that black mustang of mine.'

'I see the back of the truck's empty, Mr Williams.'

'No, it's not empty. I don't think so. There's stuff in there.'

'Those blankets you mean?'

'Yes, miss. See? Not empty. Let me remind you, I'm an upstanding citizen and member of this community, so whatever disgusting thoughts you have right now, I think you best keep them to yourself, OK?'

My grin couldn't be any wider if I tried, but I play along. 'Yes, sir. I'll try my hardest, but it's incredibly difficult when all I can think about is last night…'

I undo my top button on my shirt and open the window. I'm starting to feel the heat already and we haven't even got to the paddock yet.

It's a tough little journey. All I want to do is lean over and suck his cock as he drives. I've never been this insatiable, but I'm honestly desperate for him right now. I just want to touch and lick every inch of him. If last night taught me anything it's that I am a confident and sexual woman. I never felt like that with Alex, merely a girlfriend doing her duty, the rare times we did it anyway. Now, however, I feel like a woman in charge of her own pleasure, and I fucking like it. I want him badly, but not only that, I want to make sure he pleases me. I want to enjoy it, and I want to feel as confident as I did last night every single fucking day for the rest of my life.

With that thought, however, I start to worry. Could I risk getting attached here?

No, surely not. I laugh to myself, realising the absurdity of it. I came here to escape the clutches of a man. I don't want to fall back into that again. I'm here to train and have fun. Rebounds are fun, right, especially when you're rebounding on the ranch with a bloody cowboy? No, I definitely won't be getting attached. I need to remember what this is and that's… exactly what I need after Alex. Nothing more. Nothing less.

We pull up in front of the gates, but instead of stopping there as we did before, he tells me to, 'Stay there for a minute,' before jumping out and opening the first gateway. I like the system he has set up. It allows him to drive in without opening the gate that leads to their field, so he can drive in and out without worry of them venturing out onto the road.

When we're in there, he jumps out, closes the gate behind us and opens the one in front. We pull into the main field and he once again hops out to close the gate, showing his athleticism off to perfection before jumping back in and taking us off to the very rear of the field. I wonder where the horses are before we venture over the brow of a hill where we see them all munching away under some trees. They all look up and make their way over with a nicker or, from Onyx, a rather loud neigh. Noah pulls out some grain from behind his seat and begins to spread it near the back of the truck. Naturally, they all congregate there as he gets back inside and switches the engine on again. They all raise their heads as the truck roars to life and we start to move forward.

'So where are you taking me, Noah?'

'Just a little secluded spot I thought you might like.'

'You thought I might like or you might like?'

'I think we'll both quite like it.' His grin is the widest I've ever seen it. He's being playful and I'm finding it a real turn-on. Alex and I never had this. We never had this fun. This banter. We got on, but our relationship and the way we interacted with each other was a lot more serious and a lot more platonic than this. I guess I just didn't want to see it. Right now though, all I can see is everything I've been missing for the last few years.

Izzy would be proud of me right now, having fun and letting loose with someone who can show me a good time. Even though she was only fifteen when she passed away, she had men sussed. She'd tell me over and over again, 'Don't let them mess you around, Alice. When it comes to men, you're in charge, and make sure it stays like that.'

Being with Alex, I feel like I went back on the advice I took from her. That promise I made her. Now, however, I couldn't feel better if I tried.

Noah takes the truck through some trees, the low-hanging leaves hitting the top of the windscreen and sliding over the roof. Within seconds, we emerge into a clearing.

The view in front of me is like nothing I've seen before. It's honestly the most beautiful sight I think I may have ever seen.

Before us is a small lake. When I say small, I mean small. You can see hoof prints where the horses have wandered in and bathed or even stood and paddled to get a drink. It's beautiful, especially as the sun starts to hang low and the sky begins to turn a slight shade of red, but what catches my eye more is the picnic basket and blankets already laid out behind a small fence to the right of the lake. He's already come here and laid this out. He's put effort into this.

I can't help but let out a small, 'Wow.' And I know he's pleased with himself because he's watching me with that smile again.

'Well you sure do know how to woo a girl, don't ya?'

'Is that what I'm doing? Am I wooing you?' he asks with an edge of seriousness in his tone, as if he's asking whether I feel this is more than we originally planned or at least whether I'd be OK with that. I'm looking into this way too much and I can't. I can't afford to, because I cannot have this going any further than a bit of fun. I leave in a month and that's it. I know he doesn't want this to be any more than it already is either so I need to stop seeing what isn't there.

By the time I've shaken myself out of my thoughts, he's round by my side, door open and hand out for me to take. The look on his face is one of pure lust. He wants me as much as I want him. The scene, the effort he's gone to and all for a good shag? I could get used to this. I don't think I even got this sort of effort or attention on a special anniversary with Alex. This is new and unreal, and while walking toward the fence to climb over into this beautifully laid out space, I suddenly stop, feeling worried, anxious even that I'm not going to be able to control my emotions on this one.

'Are you OK?'

'This is a rebound, right? A bit of fun? You're not expecting anything more from me? You're not going to suddenly hate me when I *have* to leave, are you? I'm not being wrong here, having fun with you, right?'

'Listen, you said it yourself. You're on the rebound and just want to enjoy the time you're here before you have to' – he pauses, a definite hesitation – 'ya know, leave.' He looks away as he says it. He won't look me in the eye. *Stop looking into this, Alice.*

'Let's just have a little fun and enjoy ourselves. You're here to get training, which I'll give you. You'll get the best training you could have ever imagined, and we get to have a little fun while you're here, and hey, you know what they say, right? To get over one person, you need to get under another, right?' His smile is as wide as my worry was, until he spoke, his reassuring tone putting me at ease instantly, but I can't help but wonder…

'So who are you getting over?'

'I can't remember; I'm too busy getting under you.'

Well avoided there, Noah, well avoided. His brain is a mystery of information. What happened to Annabelle's mother? Why does he look as if he's been just as hurt as me? I have so many questions I want to ask, but I'm too frightened to ask them after his last outburst. I don't want to overstep the mark, especially as we're not in a relationship. Technically, he owes me no explanation, but I can't help but wonder. What did she do to him to mess him up so much?

After a quick manoeuvre over the fencing, we find ourselves opening the picnic basket under the almost fully red sky.

'Red sky at night, shepherd's delight,' I say, looking upward toward the crimson streaks currently running through the sky.

'What does that mean?'

'It's an old wives' tale really. They used to say if the sky was red like this, it would mean a good day the next day, weather wise. The other was red sky in the morning, shepherd's warning. It's usually a crock of shit, but I still think it every time I see a red sky at night.'

'Honey, any day with you is going to be a good one so it looks like it's not all wrong, right?'

We spend the next hour drinking apple juice for him and a small glass of champagne for me, along with strawberries dipped in chocolate. This stopped feeling like a fling a long time ago, but instead of worrying about it, I enjoy it, especially as we make love on top of the blankets, under the stars. It's nothing short of beautiful. The pleasure that rips through me as he goes down on me, looking up at the red clouds is something I'll never forget. I was cold while we had the picnic so he ran and grabbed me the blankets from the back of the truck. They're now thrown aside as the heat races through my body with every lick, stroke and touch of his hands.

The attention he pays me for the next hour tells me this isn't just a fling for him, and what's more worrying, I think I could fall for this man... whom I'll be saying goodbye to in just under a month's time.

*A*fter a couple of hours spent by the lake, we head into town. We need rope for the halters, and I told Noah I wanted to take another look around the shops so I know what's there in case I need anything in the next few weeks before I go home. I'm sure he winced when I mentioned going home, but again, I could just be reading into things. My mind is a complete whirl right now.

As Noah heads to the feed store, I make my way around the corner and venture along what looks like an old high street. I come across the local hairdressers and peek inside the window. There are sheets of paper in the window with prices. While I'm looking at them, I see someone out the corner of my eye make their way to the door and pop their head out to me. I automatically smile as I turn toward them, only to see *her*. My smile drops, instantly replaced with a grimace.

'Oh hi, little thing. I didn't expect to see you here alone.'

'I wasn't expecting you either.' I turn on my heels and begin making my way back to the truck, but she follows in hot pursuit.

'Honey! Honey! I'm sorry. I think we got off on the wrong foot yesterday. Can we start again? Please? I'd really appreciate it. Any friend of Noah's is a friend of mine. Please?'

While I don't know her well enough to know if she's being genuine or not, I can't help but think it's simply not worth the effort of ignoring her and having bad blood, so to speak, for the next few weeks.

'Sure, why not?' I extend my hand to shake hers and she giggles.

'Oh, so British. I love it.' She puts out her hand to meet mine and we shake. 'Hi, I'm Helen. I'm the local hairdresser. And you are?'

'I'm Alice. I'm training with Noah for the next few weeks.'

'Well ain't that something. I love those horses and what he does for them. You couldn't be training under a better person. So you're thinking about getting your hair done?'

'I wanted to yes, but I definitely don't have the time at the minute. Maybe in a couple of weeks when it's calmed down on the ranch a little?'

'Would you like to book in? I can get you in that diary?'

A new location, a new job albeit temporary and a new hairstyle go hand in hand, right?

'Sure – that sounds like a plan. I can't wait.'

I walk in with her and we find a date two weeks ahead. She pops my name in, and unlike back home where I'm given a card to remember my hairdresser and my appointment, Helen just shakes my hand. In this small town, it's pretty easy to remember who everyone is, and I can't say I hate it.

I step out of the hairdressers and find Noah looking for me.

'Hey, where have you been? I've been looking for ya.'

'Oh, were you missing me?' I tickle his chin playfully before linking arms with him as we make our way back to the truck.

'Missing you? Nahhhh.' He smiles that smile again and I melt, like I know I shouldn't, but I can't help it where he's concerned.

'I just booked a hair appointment for a couple of weeks' time.'

He stops in his tracks. 'You're getting your hair done? By Helen?'

'Yeah, why?'

'Just be careful of her, OK? She can come across real sweet, but she's anything but.'

'Are you going to elaborate on that?'

'No, you can make your own mind up, but just be careful of her, OK?'

'Sure thing, Mr Mysterious…'

I stare at him, wondering what's going through his brain right but decide not to dive any deeper. It's not my business right now. All I'm doing is getting my hair cut. How badly can that go?

ALICE – TWO WEEKS LATER

*T*he days here have whizzed past. I know they say time flies when you're having fun, but I'm not just having fun. I'm having the time of my life, discovering who I really am and what it means to experience actual joy. So time for me at the minute isn't just flying, it's like bloody Concorde and I can't seem to slow it down at all.

Noah and I have grown closer. I'm learning so much from him, it's unreal. We've now made our way through all the mustangs, working each and every one of them with some already under saddle and others slowly making their way toward having tack on. The youngsters have stolen my heart but none so much as Steve. He took to human companion-ship and everything that comes with it like a duck to water. It's as if he'd done it in a past life and remembered it all, so much so I questioned whether he actually had. Noah says that some of the mustangs have such good intuition that they know whether you're a threat or not, and when they've decided you aren't, a great deal of them just go with the flow, and that's exactly what Steve did. He just went with it as if it were the most natural thing.

Some we've sat on and others we've leant over. Noah even admitted how much easier it was carrying out his training and having someone with him who knew a little about it all. It was gratifying to know that I'm actually being a help here and not a hindrance. I'm happy knowing that he's actually enjoying my company aside from when we're in bed together, and in all honesty, I wish I didn't have to leave.

I'm falling in love with the place. Here, I'm a genuine part of the team. I'm not in Noah's shadow, despite his incredible abilities – he lets me get up front with him to experience everything just as he does, and it's what I've always wanted. To feel like a real partner and not a sideshow – in both my work life and my private life.

What isn't so good, however, is the fact that Noah and I are becoming even closer than I thought we would. Our connection is insane. His appetite for me seems never-ending, and I can't help worrying about what's going through his mind as much as the thoughts blazing through mine. Every time I mention home, he goes quiet and tries to change the subject, as if he's doing his best to ignore the pink elephant in the room.

The whole time I've been here, Alex hasn't stopped messaging me. Some are angry with me for just upping and leaving. Others he tries to say sweet things, like he misses me and he still loves me, but none seem genuine. They do nothing to me either. I don't miss him, and after these last two weeks, seeing what life can really be like, I don't feel angry anymore either. I simply feel like I've had a lucky escape.

After our usual breakfast, I wander into the barn to find Noah. He got up extra early this morning, leaving me in bed after what has become a routine of spending the night in my cabin and sneaking out early so Annabelle doesn't notice, and I can't think why. If it were the horses, he would have told me or asked me to go with him. He seemed a little agitated last night too. I wonder if he's just getting more and more anxious about my leaving but shake the thought off as soon as it enters my mind.

He's in the barn, mucking out the stables – or stalls as I now call them – with his head down.

'Hey, what ya doing? You were up super early this morning.'

'Yeah, I just couldn't sleep, that's all. How are you?'

'I'm OK, Mr Formal. You sure you're alright?'

'Yeah of course.'

'OK, well I'm taking some time off today, remember, to head into town? I'm going to get my hair done. Is that still OK?'

'You don't need to, ya know. You don't need to go get your hair cut. We could just do something together or go somewhere or even do some more training or something? I could take you to see a few things round here?'

'You could do that with me this weekend. I really want to get my hair cut. What's the big deal with going there? You hate Helen that much? I mean, I'm not massively fond of her, but Christ, it's just a haircut.'

'I don't like her, no. I don't like her knowing my business, and I don't want her to spend her whole time grilling you.'

'Well I won't tell her anything. For fuck's sake, I didn't realise you were that ashamed of shagging me, but for what it's worth, I don't usually spend my time running around telling all and sundry who I have in my fucking bed.'

With that, I throw the fork down and storm out of the barn, heading back to my cabin to get changed. Fuck this – I'll head into town now and see if she can fit me in early. Here I was worried he was getting attached when all he was ever bothered about was that people would find out. Fantastic. He's just as embarrassed of me as Alex used to me. What the fuck is so wrong with me? What's more, he's treating me like I'm some whore who's going to go shouting about her latest conquests, like I do this all the time. I'm furious right now.

NOAH

*F*uck! Why did I let her storm off like that? Why can't I handle things normally? Why can't I just tell her about my past? Why the fuck do I need to be such a closed book? Why can't I just tell her what happened?

It's surely better coming from me. Helen will tell her straight away, and then I'm fucked. She'll hate me and say I'm just as bad as him, her ex, and that she wants nothing to do with me. *Fuck!*

I throw the pitchfork down and run to her cabin, rapping on the door before stepping straight in.

'Look, we need to talk.'

'No, actually, Noah, we don't need to talk. This is just supposed to be a bit of fun. I totally get that and I understand, but let me tell you something: I'm not some whore you can keep hidden. Nor am I some outspoken slag who's going to run around town and tell everyone about *your business.* I can't believe you could make me feel so ashamed of myself. I'm honestly sick to death of arsehole men treating me like shit, and let me tell you, I won't be putting up with it anymore.

'Go get your kicks elsewhere and leave me the fuck alone.'

She grabs my jacket, which she's been wearing since she got here, and storms past me. I grab her arm, but instead of coming back to me, she turns around in a rage and tells me to, 'Fuck off and get your hands off me.'

She carries on out the cabin and heads toward the driveway, walking to the bus stop. I could go after her but my mom is on the porch. She's seen me run to the cabin. My parents know something's going on. They don't need to know about this though.

I open the now swinging screen door and step outside, watching Alice leave. Is this what it feels like to have someone you love angry at you? Because that's how I feel.

I'm falling in love with her and I know I shouldn't be, but I can't help it.

The woman consumes me, but it's still not enough, and having her angry at me right now is killing me. It's just killing me.

I make my way back toward the barn and pass my mom.

'Everything OK, son?'

'It's fine, Mom.'

'Doesn't look fine.'

I stare at her. She knows me better than anyone and she knows full well what's going on, but she doesn't know why I'm upset right now.

'She's going to get her hair cut. She's going to spend time with Helen.'

'You're worried she's going to find out?'

'Yes, ma'am.'

'Noah honey.' She takes my hand as she steps down from the porch and looks me dead in the eye. 'Life isn't black and white. It's a murky old shade of grey, and after what that girl has been through, she knows that better than just about anyone else right now. I can't say she won't find out, but if you want more from this than you're letting on then she's going to have to know one way or another. You committed no crimes. What you did wasn't right – I can't deny that, but I think looking at the bigger picture, you weren't necessarily to blame. You had a weak moment, but what happened after that *was not your fault*.

'You need to stop blaming yourself about this, and what's more, you need to stop not living your life or going after what you want because of it. I know Annabelle is your world, but she's going to grow up and head off on her own journey. What happens then? Our children should be the most important things in our lives, but that doesn't mean you stop living it. You're a good father, Noah. Living your life and being happy won't impact Annabelle negatively. If anything, it'll make her life that much better, having a truly happy father and maybe even another person who'll enrich her life even more.'

I squeeze her hand, knowing she's right, but she's told me this a thousand times before. I just can't get over my past and what I did. Every other woman in this town knows and I don't care, but she will. Alice will care. This is breaking my fucking heart.

ALICE

he bus ride to the centre of town is long and lonely. I feel like I may have overreacted, but at the same time, I've had enough of people treating me like this, like I'm worthless. Like I'm not worthy of being in the room.

I'm hoping having my hair cut will make me feel a little better. It's weird, isn't it? How a haircut can totally change the way you feel. Whenever I have my hair cut, I suddenly feel empowered. Strong enough to take on the world, strong enough to handle shit from a man like Noah.

The bus pulls up, and Gus the driver gives me the nod. He knows me from previous journeys and now gives me the nod whenever we reach my destination – a way of helping out the new girl. What's funny is that my destination never changes – I'm always heading into town to have lunch or pick up something from the feed store. I've done it about five times now in the last two weeks. I know exactly where I'm going, and even today, I'm waiting by the door because I know mine is the next stop, but he still likes to tell me. He's a sweet guy.

I jump out onto the street and wave Gus goodbye, something I'd never do back home, give the small town centre a quick glance then look toward the salon. I almost don't want to see Helen, but I need to have a little TLC and she's the one to do that here.

Turning on my heels, I start making my way to the salon. This town is quite possibly the sweetest one I've ever seen. It's tiny, but it has everything you need, and even though I've only been here a couple of weeks, I know that by the time I've got to the salon, at least five people will wave and say good morning, acknowledging me as if I've always lived here and they've always known me.

I love the way this town treats you. Everyone knows everyone, and while I guess it could feel slightly strange initially – for me anyway, who's come from something the complete opposite – I could see myself getting used to it. I get the feeling you'd be told if something strange or untoward were going on. Unlike back home, where I found out that multiple people knew what Alex was up to and chose to never tell me. They watched as I committed my life to him, putting my own passions on the back-burner, and yet they chose to say nothing. It makes for a horrid feeling.

I look down at my phone as it starts to buzz, wondering if Noah is calling me, but no. He hasn't texted, he hasn't called. Nothing. I must have hit the nail on the head with my little rant.

The name on the screen has me surprised though. It's Jen.

'Hey, you! What's wrong? You sound weird.'

'You know you have your two horses in that spare field. Do you think there's room for another two? I need to put Lincoln and Hattie somewhere quick. I don't have time to explain. I just need them out, somewhere safe. Can I throw them in there?'

'Jen, do what you want. My two are on ten acres of lush

grazing. There's more than enough room, but what's going on? And who the fuck is Hattie? Is everything OK?'

'Alice, I promise I'll explain everything when I see you. I just need to get them away from the barn.'

The she asks, 'How's the States? You met a hunky cowboy and rode off into the sunset yet?'

'Ha! Well it's funny you should say that, but it's a bit of a long story so I'll fill you in when you sound less hassled. Besides, I've gotta be out on a trail ride in like five minutes,' I lie. 'Whack Lincoln and this Hattie out with my two. It's no worries. You know the code to the key safe, right?'

'Yup, your birthday. I've got it.'

'OK, babe, stay safe, and I hope everything's OK. We'll speak soon, alright?'

'Yup, catch you soon, Alice, and thank you.'

She sounds stressed but she's one of the few people in my life that really stood by me when all the crap with Alex happened, so anything she asks for, I'm happy to give her. Besides, with her keeping her eye on Alfie and Jack too, I can only feel even better about them while I'm away. She's a real horse girl that one, through and through. Puts her boy Lincoln before everything else, but who the fuck is Hattie?

It's weird though, I feel like I can't tell her that I'm heading to get my hair cut. I said I was leaving to go train with Noah. She was so supportive, so happy for me. If I'm getting my hair cut, she'll know straight away I'm trying to make myself feel better – it's the only bloody time I step into a salon. Best to just let her think everything's fine, especially when she sounds so crap.

I reach the salon before I've had a chance to pop my phone back in my pocket and hesitate. Is Helen really that bad? If Noah's attitude today is anything to go by, maybe it's him that's the problem?

I push the door open and step in. It's empty. I'm not

surprised to be honest. With such a small town, I wonder how it stays open. The rents on these places must be so low that it still works, unlike in Brentwood, where the council is starting to buy up all the shop spaces and charge a small fortune for them.

'Hey, girl!' Helen's welcome is warm and light and instantly puts me at ease. Maybe I just need some female company and this won't be so bad after all? I won't hold my breath, but I'm trying to be optimistic.

'Hi. I know I'm super early, but I just wondered if you had a slot now? Timing wise, it just worked out better if it were this morning so I thought I'd pop in and check.' I smile, no doubt looking slightly uncomfortable because I cannot lie to save my life, and in the space of two minutes, I've lied to my best friend and someone who is essentially the town gossip. This makes me massively uncomfortable.

'I sure do – come sit yourself down.'

And just like that, the atmosphere changes. I'm not sure if this is her professional persona or whether I just felt her wrath more with a little alcohol in me last time, but she seems much nicer now. She takes me through her book of images and I point to the style I was hoping for. I want to go shorter, a clear-cut bob. My dark hair suits it, but it's been such a long time since I've actually bothered to do anything with it. Today is the day.

She puts me in the chair at her one hair-washing station and goes to town on me, massaging my scalp as she washes, conditions and then gives me a treatment. It feels wonderful. All the while, she's telling me about her town and everyone in it. She's pleasant about each individual person too... until she comes to Noah.

As soon as she starts talking about him, her tone changes.

'So how did you find out about Noah? Seems a long way to come for training?'

'Oh I've followed his career for a while now. I really enjoy the way he works, and since I split with my other half, I thought this was the perfect time to start doing some of the training he was offering. Or, I should say, his parents were offering.'

'Oh, his folks are so sweet. I've known them, and Noah for that matter, my whole life. He was married to Emily, my best friend. That's Annabelle's mother. She was a wild one. Even when she had Annabelle, she still lived life to the full.'

She wraps a soft towel around my neck, lifting my hair up and out of it while guiding me to another chair in front of a mirror.

I suddenly feel less comfortable listening to her as she starts to tell me about Emily. Especially knowing what I've been doing with Noah for the past two weeks. And now I'm looking directly at her, her softer expression seems to have changed for something slightly more smug. *Fuck's sake*. My defences want to shoot up, but instead, I say calm and inquisitive. I may not feel comfortable, but I might actually get some insight into the elusive ex of his – She Who Shall Not Be Named.

'So she was a fun woman to be around?'

'Oh absolutely, and when Annabelle came along, she was so happy. She loved being a mother. But that's when things changed between her and Noah, ya know?'

'Umm, no, not really. We've never spoken about her or about that. Trying to keep things professional. Besides, I'm leaving in a couple of weeks, so we don't really need to be getting into that.'

'Oh wow, though I can't say I'm surprised he hasn't mentioned it. I guess he's pretty ashamed of it all. I know it makes me angry when I think about it.'

Well there she goes – she's got me hook, line and sinker, hasn't she? Now I bloody want to know what's going on with the man who's been in my bed for the last two sodding weeks.

'What happened then? Why would he be ashamed to tell me?'

'Well it's not really for me to tell…'

Really, Helen? Because I think that's exactly what you're going to do, you fucking gossiping old cow.

However much I might despise her right now and wish I could simply say I'm not interested, I am. And now I really need to know.

'Well I'd love to know who I'm working for. It's only right you fill in the gaps too, instead of leaving me to assume all manner of things, right? That would be much worse.'

As if she couldn't be any more smug, her smile creeps wider and she agrees – of course she agrees. 'You're right. I should stop you from assuming something worse. Though I don't think it could get any worse, in all honesty! And us girls have to stick together, right?'

'Exactly…'

'Well it all started right after Annabelle came along. He just changed. I don't know if he was happy about being a father. Being tied down, ya know.'

'Did he start drinking or something?'

'Oh no, far worse than that. He became super controlling. Possessive. Wouldn't let her out. Wouldn't let her take Annabelle out. Always wanted her to stay on the farm, stay with the baby, but only with supervision and doing as he said. We all found it so strange and figured, ya know, a baby can bring a lot of stress and stuff, but you could see it was taking a toll on Emily. She lost a lot of weight. I'm talking that healthy baby weight you can sometimes get, ya know, a little fuller on the hips. Well she lost that and then some. The girl turned into a rake.

'He wouldn't let her out of his sight, and when he did,

she'd let loose like she'd never been out before. She needed to blow off steam being away from his clutches for a few hours, but it'd just make things so much worse when he finally found her. He kept her like a prisoner. The only time you'd see him out without her, he had the baby too, unless his parents had her. He wouldn't let her have the baby alone. It was so, so sad. Everyone used to talk around here, but of course, you wouldn't want to make things worse, so you'd say nothing most of the time.'

'Was he violent to her?' Chills run through me as I start to envision this man, a man I barely know. I'm not a huge fan of Helen, but could that be why she was so harsh with him when we first met? Though I thought they had a history?

'She used to turn up with bruises on her arms, so we suspect so, yes. But it got much worse. When she was at her lowest, ya know, withdrawn, not wanting to talk to us at all… she was left at home one night and we all saw Noah in the bar just down the road. He had Sue all over him. She's the town nuisance. Always gets herself a man, whether he's attached or not. That night he slept with Sue, behind the bar. Well, as you can imagine, with her being my best friend and all, I just couldn't stand back and watch it anymore. I told her what happened. She confronted him when he came home and he admitted everything.

'Just a few days later, she ended her life.'

I feel a cold chill run through me. Could Noah have been that controlling, that possessive that it drove her to depression? Did he really do that to her? Grinding her down, ruining her life that much that when he cheated on her, clear as day in front of their small town's residents, she couldn't take any more and ended her own life? I can't actually believe what I'm hearing.

I feel a sudden chill running through me. His arrogant

attitude when I first met him. His ability to snap and totally change his demeanour at the mere mention of her.

Could he have been trying to do the same with me and that's why he didn't want me going near Helen? Because she knew this? But wait, he said they had a history. Surely if he did all that, she wouldn't have touched him with a bargepole?

'When I spoke to Noah before, he said you guys had a history. You'd seen each other in a... umm, more than platonic sense? If he'd really done that, why did you go near him?'

'Oh, honey, he's a sweet talker. He cornered me one night in the bar, gave me some cock and bull story about her being unwell and not of sound mind. Told me how lonely he was being a single father. I'd been having such a bad day, and he said being close to me made him feel close to her, blah blah. We had a few drinks, and the sweet talking and telling me all this rubbish about her unfortunately worked. I was ashamed of myself and immediately broke it off. I'll never forgive myself for doing it, but you know what, this town can get lonely, honey. If I could take it back, I would. Especially with the way he treated me afterward. He wouldn't stop calling, wouldn't stop harassing me. Then it all came to a head when he virtually threw his daughter at me, telling her I was going to be an important person in her life.

'God, it was awful. I'll never forget it. Makes me shiver just thinking about it.'

For the rest of the cut, we sit there in silence, her asking me if I'm OK every so often, and when the silence becomes too much for her to bear, she throws on the hairdryer and drowns it out with white noise. But it isn't white noise filling my head. It's confusion and worry about who to believe and what the fuck is really going on.

I pay in silence, I walk out of the salon in silence and I ride the bus the whole way back to the ranch... in silence. What the fuck am I going to do now? Do I confront him? Do I tell him what's going on? What Helen told me? Or do I try and get the story from him and give him a chance to tell the honest truth?

I need to think, and I need to think fast, because as I turn the corner onto the drive, he's waiting for me, arse on the ground, his cowboy hat lowered over his face.

Are you really the monster she's making you out to be?

For the first time since I met him, I feel wary and I don't like feeling like that.

'Did you do it? Did you do what she said?'

He doesn't look at me, just responds calmly with, 'Well I guess that depends on what she said I did.'

I suddenly feel uneasy, like he's going to say something I don't want to hear.

'She said you were possessive. Controlling. That you ruined Emily's life, drove her to depression, stopping her from being alone with Annabelle and then you cheated on her when she was at her lowest. She said you drove her to suicide.'

He lifts his hat and places it gently on top of his head. In one swift move he's upright, brushing his jeans down. When he looks at me, he has tears in his eyes.

'I'm a good person. I don't deserve to have people talking about me or Annabelle like that, but yes, I cheated. I can't deny that. The rest of it isn't true.'

'How am I meant to believe you? Right now, you feel like a complete stranger to me.'

'Well you said it yourself, Alice, I'm just a rebound, so really, at the end of the day, does it fucking matter? You'll be on that flight in a couple of weeks, and you'll be waving goodbye to us all, so why the fuck do you care? You had a good time, right?'

He walks toward me and I stiffen. I've never seen him like this. Never seen him behave this way at all.

'I made you come. I made you come over and over and over again. You told me he'd never done that for you, so I did you a favour, right? We both got our rocks off. You got to act like a little whore for a while, and when this training is done, you get to run on home like it never happened.'

He takes another step toward me but moves around to my side, whispering into my ear, 'I get used and abused, which hey, I'm certainly not averse to, and you get to go back to being the sweet little British girl everyone thinks you are. Maybe you'll think of your cowboy rebound when you're touching yourself in your bedroom alone.'

And with that, he leaves. He walks away like the clichéd arsehole cowboy he suddenly appears to be, and I'm left behind, lost for words.

NOAH

She'd already changed the way she thought about me. I saw it in her eyes the moment she looked at me. Why let her feel confused and why let her get caught up in the shitstorm that is my personal life?

I deserve to lose her. I don't deserve to be happy. Not after what I've done. She deserves everything she ever dreamt of. I know we've grown close so the best thing I could do is make sure she isn't wanting me, or thinking about me when she goes. She needs to hate me. She needs to despise me. I don't want any doubt in her mind that I'm bad news and she had a lucky escape.

She deserves someone better. I don't deserve her.

NOAH

*A*fter spending the afternoon with Onyx and his girls, I take a slow wander back. I can't help but hate myself for the way I treated her, but I just can't risk her keeping any feelings for me. I need to ensure a clean break, but I can't deny right now, despite agreeing for this to be a rebound, I've fallen hard for her and love her too much to drag her into my sullied past.

I finally reach the main house and look toward the barn but see it's quiet. The only movement is the horses eating their hay. The horses in the corral are settled, and the evening has taken on a calm and serene feeling, though I feel anything but serene. I feel beaten. Broken.

As I stare toward Alice's cabin, a space we've spent a lot of time in over the last few weeks, I feel a tug. A pull. I'm drawn to her, but I need to back off.

'You're too late, honey…'

I look up to see my mom standing on the porch with Annabelle.

'What do you mean I'm too late?'

'Hey, Daddy, Alice isn't in there. She went out. She said

she's going to go out dancing and have some fun.'

'Well I think she deserves it after all the hard work she's been doing. Why don't you head on in and wash up before dinner?'

'OK, Daddy. But you need to woo her, OK?'

My eyebrows virtually jump above my hairline. 'Excuse me? Woo her? Are we in the 1950s still? And what do I need to do that for?'

'So you can make her your girl, of course!'

'But you're my girl!'

'Ewwww, no way. I have a boyfriend. You're my daddy! You need a girlfriend.' And with that, she moves on inside and ages about ten years right in front of me.

I glance at my feet, trying my best to avoid my mother's look, but I can't avoid her burning stare.

'She's gone out. Seems pretty angry. What happened?' Her hand sits firmly on her hip, which means she's pissed off with me.

'Helen told Alice her version of events. Basically told her I'm responsible for Emily's death. Gave her the possessive, scary, controlling rendition of the story. She'd already changed her opinion of me. She was already believing it. I figured it was for the best that I let her go. Let her believe it. She's leaving soon anyway. She doesn't need to get involved with me.'

My hands have made their way into my pockets and I'm swinging around like a tenth grader, still trying my best to avoid eye contact with my now angry mother.

'When are you going to stop punishing yourself and punishing everyone around you at the same damn time, Noah? You know she's headed out to the bar. Looks to have packed up a few things too. Annabelle said she was looking at airplanes on her phone. So I'm guessing she was looking at flights. What are you doing?'

'I don't know. I honestly don't know.'

'Well the girl doesn't know anyone in this town apart from Helen so unless you want her talking shit about you more, or worse still, getting herself in trouble with some of the men that frequent that bar, I suggest you get your ass down there and make sure she's OK and not drowning her sorrows right now.'

What the fuck am I doing? I love her. Why am I doing this?

With that, I run past my mother, kissing her cheek as I go, and head straight to the bathroom. I shower, change and get my ass in the truck as quickly as I can.

Driving there, I wonder how I'm going to approach this. After everything she's been through today, the last thing she'll want is me busting in there and making a scene.

I park up outside and make my way in. The music is on, people are enjoying themselves and she's sitting at the bar with a man on either side. She looks about as broken as I feel.

It's not long before she catches my eye, and her reaction is not a great one. She rolls her eyes and spins round, grabbing her drink and heading to the jukebox.

I stalk toward her, conscious of everyone's eyes on me, but shake it off. Fuck this town and its narrow-minded views.

'Can we talk?'

'No, Noah, we cannot talk. I'm busy having fun like the little whore I am.' Her words are already slurred. She needs to stop drinking.

She hits a button on the jukebox and brushes past me. She's as angry as she is drunk. I'd do well to back off, so I find myself a table at the back where I can keep an eye on her.

She says something to the men at the bar and they join her at the pool table. They're both pretty stoked at interacting with her, that much I can see. What I don't like are the hands all over her. She's allowing it, and every so often she catches my eye. She's making sure I can see what's going on. She's trying to get a reaction out of me or just trying to piss me off – I don't know. Either way, I'm not happy.

Her new hair looks good, but her attitude sucks. But do I deserve any better? Right now, after what I did earlier, I don't think I do. I can't help but start to feel a little anger as I watch the guys getting more and more familiar with her though.

As the night continues, she gets more and more drunk, so I speak with the bartender. We used to go to school together.

'Hey, Matty, I'm thinking young Alice has had enough to drink.'

'You said that right. I think she needs to go home or sober up – away from those two, more importantly.'

'Yeah, I know. I'm keeping an eye on her, don't worry. Just don't serve her any more.'

He gives me the nod, just like his bus-driver father Gus, and I know I'm good.

Ten minutes later, Alice stumbles toward the bar and immediately looks in my direction. She does her best impression of a sober person, trying to walk in a straight line.

'So now you're trying to control me? Helen said that's what you do. Shame I'm not your whore anymore, eh?'

I don't bite. I won't rise to it. 'I think you've had enough. Shouldn't you come home?'

'You're right, I should go home. Thankfully, I've got a flight for tomorrow. To get me the hell away from you.'

'You don't mean that.' I move closer, trying to get a grip of her arm, to hold her up if anything, but she backs off. 'Alice, we need to talk.'

'Fuck you. We don't need to say anything else. We're done. I'm having fun with these guys now.'

The taller of the two men walks toward me and grabs

hold of her waist. 'Why don't you back the fuck off, Noah? We're having fun. You don't need to be here. We'll take good enough care of her.'

'Andy, you're gonna need to back the fuck off now.' As soon as I move toward him, he backs off. Andy and his brother Drew are both useless assholes and gutless pricks to boot. They wouldn't challenge me without a beer in their gut, and even then, they're still shitting themselves.

I swoop down and grab Alice, throwing her over my shoulder.

Screaming and hitting my lower back, Alice protests as much as possible. 'Put me the fuck down. Put me down, Noah.' But I keep striding out. Straight out the front door, and I don't put her down until we reach the truck.

'What the fuck are you doing, Alice? This isn't you!'

'Maybe you don't know me. Maybe you don't know the real me, like I don't know the real you. I didn't realise I was getting involved with such a nasty piece of shit.'

The comment winds me. I feel sick, but she's drunk and going off of how I spoke to her earlier so I can't really expect anything else to come out of that potty mouth of hers.

'Just get in the truck. I'm taking you home.'

'Fuck you.'

'No, Alice, fuck you. You walked into my life and fucking turned it upside down and now, despite how I feel about you, we can't be together because of what you think of me, what the world thinks of me – hell, what I think of me. Just get in the truck. You're going to want to sleep this off.'

'Am I safe getting in here with you?' She sways, looking a little green, before spewing all over the wheel of my truck.

Fucking hell. I lift her up after wiping her mouth with my shirt and put her in the front seat. She's out cold almost immediately. I kiss her forehead and whisper, 'You're always safe with me.'

ALICE

I wake up in my cabin with a throbbing head. I have very little recollection of last night, but what I do know is that I drank far too much.

My whole body starts to throb and I carefully sit myself up. I look down and see that I'm wearing a baggy T-shirt that most certainly wasn't on me when I went out. How did I get home? Oh God, did I do something with someone last night? Surely not. Surely I wouldn't have been that reckless?

What I do remember however is that I have a plane to catch at lunchtime and need to be ready to leave. I also need to say goodbye to Tom and Brenda, as well as young Annabelle. I consider trying to do it all without having to see Noah again. I don't think I can face him.

I spend my morning rehydrating while slowly packing up my things. I have a cab coming to get me shortly so I need to say my goodbyes, and I need to do it quickly.

I drag my things out in front of the cabin and lock the front door. I gave the place a quick clean and tidy so it shouldn't be much work for Noah's mum. I don't want to leave her with more work.

She's out on the porch as I expected. I know Annabelle saw me looking at flights but I wasn't sure if she'd know what I was doing. I'm guessing she did by the sombre expression on Brenda's face.

'Hey, Brenda. Is Tom there? And Annabelle?'

'Annabelle is at school, sweetie, and my better half is taking a nap. Please don't say what I think you're going to say.' Her body sags as she looks at my bags.

'I think you know what I'm going to say. I'm sorry, but I have to leave. You know something has been going on between me and Noah, and after yesterday, I just can't stay here. I wish I could. I've fallen in love with your family. I love it here.'

'Have you fallen in love with my son?'

'I can't answer that. I have to go.'

'Before you go, I need you to take this. Noah left it. He went to Onyx to give you some space. But please read this before you board the flight, OK?'

I take the letter from her and put it in my bag. 'I'll think about it. This has been an experience I'll never forget. I can't thank you enough for everything you've done for me and the opportunity you've given me here. I wish I could stay, but I hope one day, somewhere along the line, that our paths cross again.'

I hug her tightly, holding back a sob because regardless of what happened with Noah, I'll miss her terribly. She puts her hands on my face and sniffs away her tears. She doesn't watch me get in the car – instead, she kisses my forehead and walks back in the house, shutting the door behind her.

The driver throws my things in the back of the cab and opens the door for me. With one foot in the car and my hands on the door, I take a final look around the farm before sliding in and closing the door, telling the driver to go.

We head down the long driveway. There are mustangs on

either side, enjoying the grazing that lines the long drive off the property. Just before we get to the end, I spot Steve. 'Stop!'

The car comes to a quick stop and I leap out, calling out to my favourite mustang. He whinnies and comes walking over. We've grown close, and I'm going to miss this boy a lot. He's proven to be just as much of a cheeky little shit as I expected, and I can't bear the thought of not seeing him again, but he's such a charmer, he'll find a great home. I have no doubt about that.

I slip back into the car, glassy eyed, and we drive on toward the airport. The pull of the letter in my bag is strong, and while I don't want to know what he has to say, curiosity is killing me. Should I even read it? Will it be just as nasty as he was yesterday?

I open it as we make our way onto the motorway – or *freeway* as they call it out here – and start to read…

Dear Alice,

I've never written a letter in my life, but after the way I behaved yesterday, I feel I needed to let you know what really happened and how I really feel about you.

Emily and I got together a couple of years after I left school. Everything was great at first, but she was a wild child. Too wild for me. We split up and got back together in our late twenties. She still liked to party, but I figured that was just her nature and something I needed to accept. After a while, the booze wasn't enough anymore and she started experimenting with other ways to get her kicks.

I didn't know that drugs had become such a big part of her life and only found out when it was too late. She was addicted to drugs, mostly cocaine, but her substance of choice got stronger as her addiction grew deeper. I tried to get her help, and for a while, she looked like she was getting better. Our relationship got better and we married. She fell pregnant with Annabelle and my life was complete... until Annabelle was born and the drugs began calling all over again.

I tried my best to keep her away from them, keep her away from the temptation, and as a result, became very controlling. I desperately tried to stop the drugs taking hold, and with her refusing to seek help, I felt like there was nothing I could do. I couldn't kick her out. She was Annabelle's mother. So we kept her on the farm as much as possible and just tried to manage her addiction.

Every so often, she'd leave and let loose in the very same bar you did last night. I hate that place because of the amount of times I had to go get her and drag her ass back home. She'd be high as a kite and I'd have to take her back to the farm and try to keep her away from Annabelle, who at the time was just six months old.

It took a toll on me. I wasn't strong enough to deal with it. In fact, I was weak. I gave her medication from the doctors one night. She was out of it, sleeping. I left Annabelle with my parents and went to the bar. I wanted to see if I could find the men who I suspected were supplying her, but instead I fell into the arms of Helen. I slept with her that night. I needed attention. I needed an escape. I shouldn't have done it, but I was anything but in my right mind.

I did what I did and I can't take that back. The guilt took hold of me. I couldn't keep it a secret anymore. I had to tell her, so I did. Not long after, she overdosed again and this time, it was too much for her body to take.

Helen was telling you what she wanted you to hear. She knew full well about Emily and her addictions. But we decided not to correct others in the town simply for Annabelle. I don't want her to find out about her mum's overdose. We told her she had an illness. I'm sure that when she's older, she'll find out more, but that's a bridge I'll cross when I come to it.

I love you more than you'll ever know. I know we said this was a casual thing, but I fell in love with you. I couldn't help it. The way I spoke to you yesterday was quite simply my way of pushing you away. I didn't mean what I said; I just wanted you to stay away from me. You don't deserve to be stuck with a guy like me. You deserve the very best. I am not worthy of you, and that's why I did what I did.

I'm not the most eloquent of men, but I hope you understand what I've written, what really happened and where I'm coming from. I'll never forget you. You quite simply changed my life.

Yours always,

Noah xx

My eyes are filled with tears. Why wouldn't he just tell me that in the first place? Why would he keep that hidden from me?

'We need to turn the car around. I need to go to the paddocks on 5th and Main Street. Please. Can we change direction now?'

'Yes, ma'am. Sure can.'

The cab driver does what is without a doubt an illegal U-turn and I couldn't be more thankful.

After five minutes of driving, I can see the corner paddock and the gate to Onyx's field. As soon as the driver pulls up, I throw some notes at him and jump out of the cab, asking him to wait, just in case. I can see Noah's truck in the middle of the field and his boots poking out of the driver's door.

I slam the cab door shut and see him move. He must have heard it. The letter is in my hand as I run and jump the gate, sprinting up the hill toward him. He's just standing there, not moving toward me. My heart is racing as I near him. He looks glassy eyed. He's been crying.

'This letter – did you mean what you said in this letter?'

'Every damn word.'

'You're in love with me?'

'I know we said it wasn't going to be serious—'

'I didn't ask that – I asked if you're in love with me?'

Walking toward him, so I can look him deep in his soul as he gives me my answer, I ask one more time, 'Are you in love with me, Noah? Did you mean what you said?'

'Yes. I'm in love with you, Alice.' He looks broken but he needn't be.

'I wish you'd just told me what happened from the very beginning.'

'I know.' He takes my hand and slowly moves closer, closing the already small distance between us. 'But I couldn't. The way I treated you yesterday was disgusting but I just needed to make sure that you wouldn't want to be with me. I don't deserve you. You deserve someone who can give you a life with no baggage, no small-town gossip.'

'What if I just want someone who loves me?'

'You deserve better.'

'I deserve you. Noah, I know I said this was a rebound, a fucking fling – but I'm in love with you too. I don't know how the hell we're going to work this, but I'm in love with you, and all I need to know right now is whether you want to give this a shot or not?'

Instead of speaking, he kisses me – hard. And with that I know my rebound on the ranch has become something much more. I have no idea how we're going to make this work, but what I do know is that I want it so bad. I want him. My cowboy. My Noah. My love.

ACKNOWLEDGEMENTS

Well, what can I say apart from the fact that it's been a minute since you last read one of my acknowledgement pieces. I published my first novella in September 2020 in the middle of a global pandemic and boy was it tough, but not as tough as creating a follow up to the Soaked Hay series.

What is it they say? Everyone has a book in them but I didn't know that I would have three, or even more. I have so much planned for 2022 but before I get too excited about that, I just want to see how far this little treasure goes. It was so much fun writing this story. I imagined the opening chapter for a long time, and wondered where I would take it, why Noah would be the way that he is and how I could still make him loveable.

I've spent so many nights planning out this story, along with the two follow up books (yup you heard me right, there are two more books in this series), that writing it became harder than ever. I had such a vision in my head of where things were going but as happened with my first two books, as soon as the words started hitting the page, the story took on a mind of its own and became something entirely different.

I've taken a lot of inspiration in the last 12 months from some of my favourite TV series. Inspiration in the sense that I need to stop worrying about the story, what I'm writing and simply write it because the story needs it, not because it sits well within my genre. I believe that my readers will find me for the stories I write and I guess if you're reading this, you did - you found me.

As this is an acknowledgement piece however, it's about time I actually acknowledged those who really made a difference in the entire process. Of course, I couldn't have done any of this without the help of my own leading man, Rob. He is quite possibly the most supportive partner possible, giving me the space I need (and cooking all the meals) so I can put words on a page. He even reads my writing, chapter by chapter telling me where I need to change lines, catching my inevitable spelling mistakes as excitement rushes me through a paragraph - mindlessly at times.

I also need to say a huge thank you to my two little girls, who are a little less little than they were when I began this journey they call writing. They've become so used to 'Mummy working' which has caused many a teary moment of 'mum-guilt' but at the same time, has made me so proud to see how thrilled they are that 'Mummy wrote a book'. My girls are the reason for everything, the reason for the late nights, the reason for the bags under my eyes (which unfortunately are not Chanel). They're my reason and will always be my reason and while I may work toward making a more secure future for them, I know it doesn't come without it's sacrifices. Maybe one day they'll read this and know I did it all for them… one day.

I also want to thank my parents, for buying my books and

promising to never read them because let's face it, that would be bloody awkward.

I must also say a huge thank you to Laura Kincaid for the incredible editing yet again and the wonderful Francessca Wingfield for her amazing cover design - both of you were flawless as always.

Last but not least, I'd like to thank you, my readers. Without whom I wouldn't be able to carry on doing this, wiring my stories. I hope you enjoy reading the story of Alice & Noah as much as I enjoyed writing it. Do stay in touch and let me know what you thought. Until then, keep reading guys!

Cover Design: Francessca Wingfield - https://www.facebook.com/FrancesscasPRandDesigns
Editing: Laura Kincaid - https://www.tenthousand.co.uk/
Tea Maker: Rob Hyde - www.fitfob.com

WHAT'S COMING NEXT?

You'll be pleased to know that this isn't the end of the road for Alice & Noah. In fact, there is plenty more to come in this romantic adventure on the ranch!
Keep your eyes peeled for the next in the series, Romancing On The Ranch; to be swiftly followed by Ride Away On The Ranch. I hope you've enjoyed getting to know these guys, especially for those who read my first two novellas and guessed that this book would focus on the elusive Alice.

Get to know me more here…
Instagram - https://www.instagram.com/thefairweatherrider/

Facebook - https://www.facebook.com/thefairweatherrider
Website - http://thefairweatherrider.com

WANT TO READ MORE FROM FW RIDER?

Want to read more from me? Check out more works below...

Soaked Hay & Farrier Smoke
Soaked Hay & Stable Mirrors

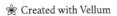 Created with Vellum

Printed in Great Britain
by Amazon

68750838R00073